Juneau Black

Cold Clay

Juneau Black is the pen name of authors Jocelyn Cole and Sharon Nagel. They share a love of excellent bookshops, fine cheeses, and a good murder (in fictional form only). Though they are two separate people, if you ask either one a question about her childhood, you are likely to get the same answer. This is a little unnerving for any number of reasons.

Cold Clay

Cold Clay

A SHADY HOLLOW MYSTERY

Juneau Black

VINTAGE CRIME / BLACK LIZARD

Vintage Books

A Division of Penguin Random House LLC

New York

FIRST VINTAGE CRIME / BLACK LIZARD EDITION, MARCH 2022

Copyright © 2017 by Jocelyn Koehler and Sharon Nagel

All rights reserved. Published in the United States by Vintage Books,
a division of Penguin Random House LLC, New York, and distributed in
Canada by Penguin Random House Canada Limited, Toronto.
Originally published in paperback in the United States by
Hammer & Birch LLC, Philadelphia, in 2017.

Vintage is a registered trademark and Vintage Crime / Black Lizard
and colophon are trademarks of Penguin Random House LLC.

Library of Congress Cataloging-in-Publication Data
Name: Black, Juneau, author.
Title: Cold clay / Juneau Black.
Description: First Vintage Crime / Black Lizard edition. | New York :
Vintage Books, a division of Penguin Random House LLC, 2022. |
Series: The Shady Hollow mystery series ; 2.
Identifiers: LCCN 2021032413 (print)
Subjects: GSAFD: Animal fiction. | Thrillers (Fiction).
Classification: LCC PS3602.L293 C65 2022 (print) | LCC PS3602.L293 (ebook) |
DDC 813/.6—dc23
LC record available at https://lccn.loc.gov/2021032413

Vintage Crime/Black Lizard Trade Paperback ISBN: 978-0-593-46628-5
eBook ISBN: 978-0-593-46629-2

Book design by Christopher M. Zucker

www.blacklizardcrime.com

Printed in the United States of America
10   9   8   7   6   5

Author's Note

Cold Clay is a tale of woodland creatures, set in the village of Shady Hollow. From time to time the contemplative reader may pause to question the spatial mysteries that allow a mouse and a moose to frequent the same establishments, or wonder at the civility among foxes and rabbits, creatures so often placed at opposite posts on the spectrum of predator and prey. A skeptic with an eye for minutiae may even ask why a rat requires a visit to the haberdasher. In turn, we ask such skeptics to look to their own hat collections before passing judgment on another.

We remind our gentle readers that this is a work of fiction, and the characters' resemblance to real creatures is superficial indeed. If it assists with your quandary, we suggest you think of the characters merely as humans with particularly animalistic traits . . . and haven't we all met such folk?

With that guidance, we cordially invite you to return to Shady Hollow.

Cast of Characters

Vera Vixen: *This cunning, foxy reporter has a nose for trouble and a desire to find out the truth, no matter where the path leads.*

Chief Theodore Meade: *Bears make excellent law enforcers: big, brawny, and belligerent. But Chief Meade seems singularly uninterested in solving crime when he could be fishing.*

Deputy Orville Braun: *This large brown bear is the more hard-working half of the Shady Hollow constabulary. He works by the book. But his book has half the pages ripped out.*

BW Stone: *The cigar-chomping skunk of an editor of the Shady Hollow* Herald. *BW ("Everything in black and white!") loves a good headline.*

Lenore Lee: *A dark-as-night raven who opened the town's bookshop, Nevermore Books, and has a penchant for mysteries.*

Joe Elkin: *This genial giant of a moose runs the town coffee shop, the local gathering spot. If gossip is spoken, Joe has heard it—but this time he is the gossip.*

Joe Elkin Jr.: *Joe's only son and his pride and joy. But Joe Junior's childhood was less sunny than one might wish.*

Julia Elkin: *Joe's wife, who walked out on him years ago and was never heard from again.*

Octavia Grey: *This striking mink is the town's newest resident. She excels at etiquette and knows how to turn heads.*

Gladys Honeysuckle: *As the town gossip and busybody, there's nothing Gladys doesn't know. She hates to be scooped on a juicy tidbit.*

Sun Li: *This panda is a former surgeon and a current chef. He runs the Bamboo Patch, a restaurant serving vegetarian dishes to die for.*

Howard Chitters: *Once a humble accountant and now the de facto head of the sawmill, Chitters is an object lesson in how murder can shake up a routine.*

Esmeralda von Beaverpelt: *The daughter of the town's once-richest family is now a hardworking waitress at Joe's Mug. Esme is good with numbers and even better with money.*

Anastasia von Beaverpelt: *Esme's snobby sister still hasn't adjusted to the family's changed circumstances. And everybody in town knows it.*

Edith von Beaverpelt: *Widow, business owner, and philanthropist Edith loves her daughters and hates a scandal.*

Barry Greenfield: *A senior reporter at the* Herald, *this old hare has seen it all, and he remembers it all, too.*

Lefty: *A small-time criminal, this masked raccoon lives in the shadiest part of Shady Hollow. He's got a heart of gold (just don't ask where he got it).*

Ambrosius Heidegger: *Professor of philosophy and general know-it-all. The owl is the smartest creature in the forest and never lets anyone forget it.*

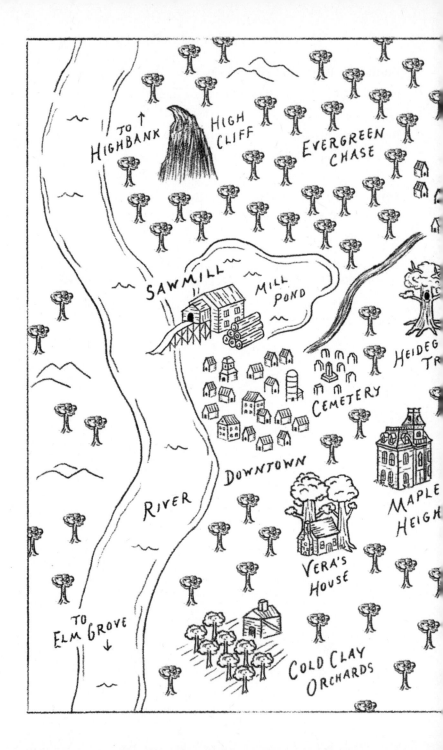

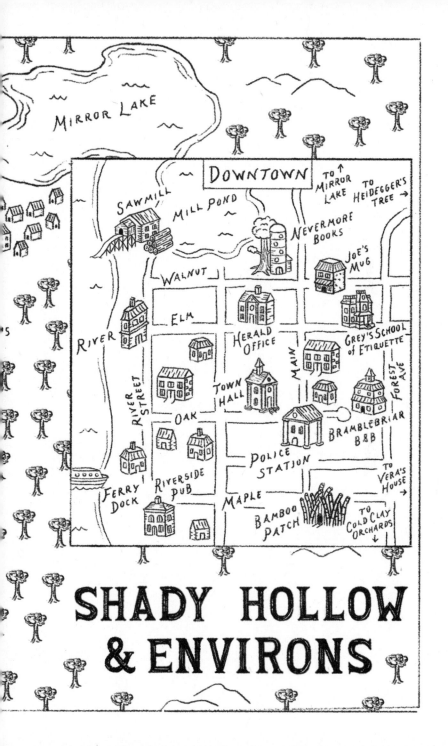

Cold Clay

Chapter 1

As might be expected from its name, the village of Shady Hollow is nestled deep in the woods, covering a wide valley between two mountains. What might be less expected is the fact that the village residents are all animals, representing many species and temperaments. Just *how* can a rabbit live and work alongside a fox? *Why* do a sparrow and a bear read the same newspaper? On a more practical level, *where* are the rabbit and fox working, and *what* is the headline on the paper?

These are the sorts of questions a journalist asks. In her den, Vera Vixen was in fact asking herself exactly what the headline would be for the next issue of the Shady Hollow *Herald* and whether she could improve it. She loved the little town, but it usually was not the most exciting place in the world. Vera wasn't sure she could handle looking at another headline like "Mirror Lake Beach Closes Early" or "Best Walking Paths in the Whispering Woods." Those were not ledes to inspire.

"There must be something worth writing about today," she muttered. "I just have to find it."

As Vera prepared to leave her cozy home, she pulled a woolen scarf off a hook by the door and draped it about her shoulders, pleased with the way the deep evergreen color contrasted with her rich red fur. She adjusted the wire-rimmed glasses on her nose, tipped her felt hat to a slightly jauntier and more *reporterish* angle, and then stepped outside to greet the day.

The early-autumn mornings were rather chilly now, and quite often a layer of fog would slip into town at night, slinking through the quiet streets and curling up around the great trees in the park. Early risers had to brave a clinging mist that hid the details of the world, making Shady Hollow seem like a dream of itself. But soon the sun would rise over the distant ridge and burn away the fog until the last ragged strips retreated into the woods as the town bustled into action and animals emerged from houses and dens to begin their work or play. On this day, the fog was behaving in the most picturesque way possible, and Vera smiled as she breathed in the cool air. Despite the calm, she felt a thrill of excitement that only an autumn morning can supply. Something about the brisk air and the golden tips of the tree branches warned of change to come. But what sort of change? Ah, that was the question!

She trotted along the path toward the center of town, where the newspaper office could be found. When she crossed an intersection, a flurry of activity on the other end of Elm Street caught her eye. She paused for a longer look. A large covered cart stood parked in front of one of the empty buildings. Ferrets scurried about, carrying boxes and bags from the cart and nearly colliding with one another as they passed through the building's narrow doorway.

Vera's interest was piqued. That building had been for rent for some time; its first-floor office had been looking lonely and drab on the otherwise busy street. Vera knew the upstairs was very large, but she'd never been inside. Someone must have taken out a lease on the place, and it must be a newcomer. A local would have mentioned it by now.

"Excuse me," Vera called, addressing the ferrets, who didn't look away from their work. "Excuse me!" She trotted closer, pausing just short of the commotion.

One ferret finally stopped, looking at her in alarm. "Hello, yes, what? We didn't break anything! Promise! We have a no-break guarantee."

"I just wanted to know who's moving in," Vera explained.

The ferret shook his dark head. "Can't tell you. Sorry! We just move the freight."

"But who's paying you? You must know that!" she said. "Where did the shipment come from?"

"Freight moved upriver, ma'am," the ferret said, shrugging to convey his complete lack of knowledge in the matter. "Payment in cash. Sorry! Watch that lamp!" The last direction was howled at another ferret who seemed about to lose control of a fancy blown-glass lamp. Vera's interlocutor dashed past her to save the object from being smashed to a thousand pieces on the ground.

Vera took the hint and didn't ask anything further of the workers. She would have loved to hang about and peek at the belongings of the town's newest resident for clues as to their identity, but now she had to get to the office. She couldn't wait to see if she had scooped Gladys Honeysuckle, the town gossip.

What would this new resident bring to Shady Hollow? Vera had learned that even in a small town, you just never know what could happen. Despite her annoyance with the current milquetoast headlines, Vera had no desire to revisit the shocking events of the summer and her own narrow escape from death. Never before had the residents endured the horror of not one but two murders. The investigation had temporarily shut down the sawmill—the town's largest employer and the lifeblood of the local economy. Vera chased the story of the killings a little too eagerly, and she was lucky she was still alive to grouse about the latest lack of news.

She paused on seeing a copy of the day's paper on a stoop. "'Summer's Over for Mirror Lake Beach,'" she read out loud. "Called it."

A second later, she sighed. She should be happy. Things had returned to normal, at least outwardly. Creatures had resumed their routines, and gossip about regular life had recommenced. It was better to hear complaints about the neighbors' decorating choices rather than whispers about murder and infidelity.

"Something the matter, Miss Vixen?" a deep voice rumbled behind her.

Vera turned to see Deputy Orville Braun standing there, looking quite professional in his uniform and cap, though with a rather *un*professional twinkle in his eye. She had to look up to catch the twinkle, since the brown bear was so tall in comparison to her.

She smiled at him. "Nothing other than a little ennui."

"Ennui? I've heard coffee and morning rolls can fix that,"

Orville said. "I'd be honored if you would join me at Joe's. I'll escort you there safely," he added.

"No doubt!" Vera said with a laugh as they started walking down the street together. Not that there was any danger at the town's favorite coffee shop. In fact, ever since Orville helped save Vera's life not long ago, he'd shown a lot of concern for her safety, walking her home from work, seeing that she ate well during her recovery, buying her flowers to keep her spirits up . . . Or perhaps that was the result of the fact that they had started dating. Not more than the occasional dinner and evening stroll, but Vera had to admit that her feelings for Orville were growing by the day.

They were taking things slowly, but Vera looked forward to their dinners. It was great fun to have someone to dress up for, and it put a spring in her step during the rest of the week. She had almost stopped looking over her shoulder wherever she went.

When they reached Joe's Mug at the corner of Main and Walnut, Orville held the door open for her.

She walked in, waving to Joe, who stood behind the counter.

"Look who's here," said the proprietor. Joe was a huge, genial moose who always had a smile for a visitor. "Miss Vixen, with none other than our good deputy."

"We just happened to meet on the sidewalk," Vera said quickly, because it was rather early in the day.

"And I imagine you both are feeling a bit peckish." Joe nodded his huge head toward a booth, inviting them to sit.

Vera slid into the booth, and Orville sat opposite her, both of them steadfastly ignoring the other morning customers, all of whom were quite aware of their budding romance.

Only when Joe brought two mugs and a coffeepot did Vera

glance around the café at her neighbors. Absolutely no one would believe that she and Orville had run into each other by accident. Whispers of an assignation would spread around Shady Hollow like wildfire. Yes, the residents needed something new to gossip about. Vera most definitely did not want that something to be Orville and her, but there was little she could do about it.

"Couple of those morning rolls, too, please," Orville told Joe. "The ones with the pecans."

"Coming right up, Deputy!" Joe gave a little salute and ambled away.

"So . . . Deputy," Vera said. She was behaving as if they barely knew each other, which was silly but instinctive. Constant scrutiny by one's neighbors was one of the downsides of living in a small village. In the city, no one would have noticed if she and Orville went on dates every day, but here in Shady Hollow nothing was missed. "You must be enjoying the calm."

"I really can't say that I am." Orville glanced briefly out the window toward the street, which was slowly filling with folks on their way to work or school. "The chief is away, and someone has to mind the store. But there's not much to mind. I knew I could leave the station to get a quick bite. It's too early in the day for crime! Though not too early for fishing," he added with only a trace of annoyance.

Vera refrained from muttering about the chief slipping away from work to fish and smiled at her companion. If Orville wanted to maintain the illusion that Chief Meade ran the police department, who was she to say any differently? It was an open secret among the townsfolk. Still, she wondered at Orville's patience with the chief. She hadn't quite worked up the nerve to ask why he put up with Chief Meade's lackadaisical efforts.

The morning rolls Orville had requested arrived at the table, and Vera temporarily forgot her trail of thought as she pulled apart the delightfully sticky bread and nibbled away.

"Do you know anything about the new tenant on Elm Street?" she asked after licking the toffee from her paws. "I saw the movers this morning."

Orville shook his head. "I noticed the for-rent sign had come down from the window a few weeks ago, but I thought perhaps Mr. Blakely had just given up for the rest of the year. It's good news if someone leased the place. It's too big and drafty to sit empty, and it made the street feel too quiet."

Vera knew that Orville had a uniquely safety-oriented view on town matters, and a vacant structure rarely looked safe.

"It is a big space," she agreed. "I wonder what the new business will be."

"Check the town hall's records. All commercial ventures need to be registered and approved by the council." Orville had been a cop in Shady Hollow long enough to know the rules.

Vera was annoyed by her own lapse in knowledge. "If it was approved, why didn't the council say so?"

"Oh, there's a three-month window," he explained. "Lets new owners get things started, you see. Shows the council the business is going to succeed. Or not. Either way, the votes aren't a surprise."

"Ah." That made Vera feel better.

Just then, Joe ambled over and placed two bowls of warm applesauce on the table. "On the house. No better way to start an autumn morning," he said in his low, rumbling voice.

Vera inhaled the scented steam with delight. "Oh, that's grand." She prepared to take a bite of what she already knew would be a perfectly spiced spoonful. The tang of apples and the warmth of cinnamon and cloves made her sigh happily. "Made fresh. I can tell."

"Very first of the season," Joe responded. "There will be a lot more coming. Timothy says the bulk of the harvest is just ripening now. I expect they'll be busy this week up at Cold Clay."

The Leveritt family had managed Cold Clay Orchards for generations—which wasn't saying much, because the Leveritts were rabbits. The orchards and berry patches had provided superior crops for many years. Vera hoped they'd continue to do so for decades more.

"Tim told me he hired extra pickers this year," Joe went on. "Planting all those new varieties paid off. He's doing good business. He must be pleased with his crop."

Later Vera would recall Joe's words with a shiver, because the orchards were about to reveal a most unexpected and unwelcome harvest.

Chapter 2

The owners of Cold Clay Orchards took their work seriously, and the orchards produced choice fruits from spring through the first snowfall. Early in the year, berries were plentiful and plump. In high summer, peaches and pears ripened and were turned into sweet delights in the oven. But in fall . . . well, that was when apples were in season. Glorious apples. Red, green, yellow! Sweet and tart, crisp and juicy.

Fall was the busiest time at Cold Clay Orchards.

That day, when the breeze turned cool and the air was scented with apples, a crew of about twenty apple pickers gathered for work. This was pleasant work if you could get it—staying outside all day in the bright sunshine instead of being cooped up inside. Most of the rabbits looked forward to the time when they could make extra money for something they already enjoyed doing.

Timothy Leveritt was in charge of the harvest this autumn, just as he'd been for years. He made most of the day-to-day decisions regarding staffing, planting, and delivering products to customers. However, the orchard was a collective, owned equally by all the rabbits who worked there. Only a few were lucky enough to work at Cold Clay year-round, since fruit was most definitely a seasonal business.

"All right, let's get to work!" Timothy pointed to the pile of wooden baskets used for the apple harvest, then to the particular rows of trees. "I want half of you lot on the row with the Newton Reds, and the other half harvesting the Sunsets. Whichever team fills the most baskets by noon gets a bonus!"

As the crew began to grab the baskets, Timothy said to a couple of the rabbits standing closest to him, "Peter and Ralph, you're on special duty. That one tree at the end of the Sunset row needs to be dug up and replaced. It's never thrived like the rest, and this year was worse than ever. I want it out of the ground and replaced so we can start fresh next season. Shovels and picks are by the trunk."

Peter and Ralph nodded smartly and headed to the far end of the long row of trees. Most limbs were heavy with apples. The skin of each fruit was a remarkable blend of red and a rosy orange, giving the Sunsets their name.

"Can't wait for the first pie made with these," Ralph commented as they went. "I remember when Tim brought these saplings in. What—ten, eleven years ago now? No one had heard of a Sunset apple. Now they're the top variety."

Peter nodded in agreement. He was a quiet creature by

nature and had nothing to add to Ralph's statement. It was pleasant in the dappled shade of the trees, and that was enough for him.

Sadly, this particular day would end less pleasantly than it began. The two rabbits each took a shovel and began to dig around the roots of the ailing apple tree. The ground here was hard to work, the end of the row being less tended than other parts of the orchard.

A half hour or so brought progress; the rabbits had dug themselves into a pit of sorts surrounding the large root ball of the apple tree. They took a break, feeling the heat of the sun on their fur.

"What I wouldn't give for a cool cider right now," Ralph said.

Peter nodded in wholehearted agreement, then sighed and picked up his shovel once more.

He stopped working abruptly when his shovel struck something hard. He looked down and saw something white at his feet. Bending down, he brushed dirt away from the object. This wasn't a tree root or a stone. It was . . .

"Is that a bone?" Ralph asked, having noticed Peter's work.

"Think so," Peter said, brushing away yet more dirt. "Quite a big one, too." He popped his head out of the hole and looked around. All the other workers were still down at the opposite end of the row, climbing ladders and tossing apples into baskets, happily going about the day's work.

Ralph followed the line of the bone and started digging at one end. His shovel struck something, too, and he shortly uncovered another bit of pale bone. He said, in a troubled tone, "We'd better get Leveritt over here to see. And then send someone to fetch the police."

Chapter 3

Orville and Vera had just stepped outside onto the street after breakfast when a harried-looking rabbit bounded up the road toward them.

"Deputy! Deputy!" The rabbit skidded to a halt, panting.

"What's wrong?" Orville asked, looking in the direction the rabbit had come.

"You've got to see, sir. Up at the orchards. Follow me!"

Vera's ears perked up, sensing a story. "I'm joining you," she announced to Orville.

"We don't even know what's happened," the bear replied. "Could be dangerous."

"Well, it will be less dangerous with a deputy of the law by my side," Vera countered.

On their way over to Cold Clay Orchards—the messenger had already run ahead of them—they speculated about what the problem could be.

"He sounded so upset," Vera noted. "They must have found something bad to have run for the law."

"Or they're just trying to prevent something worse," said Orville. "Maybe they found a drunk vagrant on the orchard property—that's happened a time or two. Or one of the workers stole another's lunch bucket."

But Vera doubted it was something so simple. The panic in the rabbit's eyes suggested something worse.

"Whatever it is, Vera, remember that I'm the one they called. You can observe from a distance, but don't interfere. Understand?"

"Of course!" Vera nodded her head vigorously. She knew better than to step on Orville's toes while he was working. She hated when other folks did it to her.

The orchard was in an uproar when the pair arrived. The apple pickers were standing in clusters, pulling at their ears in that way rabbits do when they're nervous. They were whispering and pointing at a pile of disturbed earth. Vera recognized Timothy Leveritt, who had rushed over to Orville the moment he saw the deputy.

"Hey there, Deputy," Timothy said, eyes darting between both Orville and Vera. "Could you please step over here?" He indicated the loose dirt.

Orville and then Vera moved to the hole to look at an extremely *large* skeleton, which Ralph was now patiently exposing with a trowel and a whisk broom.

"That's not good," Orville grunted.

Murmurs began anew among the observers. Timothy put

a stop to the mumbling with some quick orders: "Ralph, why don't you stop digging and step away from the, er—the bones. Let the deputy examine things. Everyone else, get back to work. Those apples won't pick themselves."

The crew moved away, although slowly, backing up as a group, as if they each didn't want to miss anything. They went back to the trees they had been picking, but no one started their work again. They merely stared at the site of the grisly discovery from a farther, safer distance. The sounds of muttering and speculation drifted toward Orville and Vera on the light breeze. Vera looked up at the sky, where puffed clouds appeared in the deep, startlingly clear blue. It was entirely too beautiful a day for such a sad event.

Orville climbed down into the hole, peering closely at the exposed bones.

"What do you think?" Vera called. She was itching to jump down there, too, but she knew Orville wouldn't take kindly to being crowded.

The bear looked up at her. "This is going to take a while. I should get someone out here to look at the skeleton."

"What was it? What sort of creature, I mean?"

"Can't tell. Something big. Bear, maybe," he added with a shiver. "Whatever it was, this creature has certainly lain here undisturbed for a long time. It's not recent."

"So that's . . . good?" If a large creature had gone missing near Shady Hollow, everyone would have heard about it. So it made sense that these bones had been here awhile. But why were they here at all, instead of, say, in the cemetery?

"Vera, ask Tim to send someone to fetch Dr. Broadhead, please. He's in town today, luckily."

She turned away from the scene to seek out Timothy Leveritt. He immediately pulled aside one of his workers, a sleek brown rabbit named Dahlia, and passed on the message.

"Tell her to come right back," Vera added. "Don't let her talk to anyone in town besides the doctor. Try to keep the rest of your workers here, too. I'm sure Deputy Orville will want to speak to everyone." In reality, Vera didn't want news of the discovery to spread before she could at least write up a short article about it. She flipped to a fresh page in her notebook and started writing her impressions of the scene.

Orville's first step was to cordon off the hole with a rope supplied by the orchard's workers. There were rabbits everywhere, and he didn't want any creature disturbing the evidence.

"Maybe the animal died of natural causes and a loved one buried them here in the orchard for some unknown reason," Vera suggested from where she stood at the edge of the wide hole. A large skull lay partially revealed. She squinted but couldn't tell to what creature it might have belonged.

"Maybe." Orville sounded distant. "We can't make guesses until we have more evidence. The *Big Book of Policing* is very clear about that." Orville was referring to a large dog-eared tome that sat in the police station and stayed generally undisturbed until times of crisis.

"What's it say about finding bones?" she asked.

"To not disturb them." Orville looked up at her. "I don't remember what it says about dealing with nosy reporters. How about you step away from the scene, Vera? Please. This is probably just an old body that's been here for decades."

With a huff, Vera retreated to a shady spot under an apple tree on the other side of the grassy row. Unlike the police bear, she was hoping the story would be just a bit more interesting than old, unidentifiable bones. She felt a spark of excitement when she considered the possibilities of the story she could write. She was no doctor, but she had eyes, and she was fairly certain that she had seen signs of damage to the skeleton's skull before she had been so quickly banished.

The sun rose higher, warming the air. Vera interviewed all the workers she could, writing down their reactions to the discovery in her notebook.

There was a flurry of activity among the spectators as Dr. Broadhead arrived. He was a long copper-colored adder possessed of keen intelligence and the sort of gaze that made most creatures a bit nervous. Though the snake was well known for his excellent work and certainly was a civilized creature, there was a little something off-putting about him. Vera thought it was the fact that a snake's facial expressions just didn't look right. You could never tell if a snake was happy or angry or . . . hungry.

"They sssaid I wasss requesssted." Dr. Broadhead slithered through the grass toward the deputy, who was now standing just next to the grave.

"We found bones. Very large bones." Orville pointed to the hole. "I need to know whatever you can tell me about them."

The medical examiner nodded at Orville but said nothing more. He merely made his way under the rope marking the section as off-limits to nonofficial folks—not a difficult task for a snake—and approached the skeleton. Vera edged forward, giving in to her desire to see what was happening.

Dr. Broadhead slid over the many exposed bones and coiled his tail around several, assessing their size and density. He made little hissing sounds—*"Yesss," "Interesssting,"* and *"Sssingular"*— as he worked. When he got to the skull, he threaded one eye socket with his tail and held the whole thing aloft, peering at it with unblinking black eyes.

After this careful observation, he put the skull down gently and returned to Orville.

"What was it? A bear?"

Dr. Broadhead swayed side to side. "No. A perusssal of the bone sssizesss isss definitive. There isss only one creature in the woodlandsss with a femur larger than the mighty brown bear'sss. That creature isss the moossse."

Chapter 4

A moose?" Orville looked both flummoxed and relieved. No creature liked to look at its inevitable fate quite so baldly. "How long ago did it die?"

Dr. Broadhead let out a gentle hissing sigh. "Yearsss ago. I will be able to be more precsssissse when I run sssome tessstsss on the bonesss in my laboratory. I will not sssay anything about the caussse of death until I have exsssamined everything more carefully."

Vera was not at all surprised to hear this sort of statement from Dr. Broadhead. The snake was good at his job and always very careful not to speculate until he had exhausted all other options.

Orville thanked the examiner for coming so quickly and then turned to Vera. "It looks like I will be transporting the bones to the doctor's office. Might be a while before we know anything more. I expect you'll have an article written before the day is out."

"It's news, even if we don't know the details yet," Vera said, nodding, "and I better get this typed up. See you later, Orville."

Vera decided she had learned all she could at the scene, at least for the moment. She headed back to town. But instead of going to the newspaper office, she took a quick detour to Nevermore Books, where her best friend, Lenore, could be found most days. Vera had a hunch.

The bookstore stretched taller than all the buildings around it—in fact, it was a repurposed granary. Though it now sat on one of the major intersections of Shady Hollow, the silo had been "in the country" when it was built, well out of the way of the hustle and bustle of the main streets. The tall, narrow structure had held grain throughout the winter months. Eventually, it was no longer needed, and the growing town meant that farmland had moved farther out. The granary was too big to pull down, so it merely sat for years, a symbol of the town's past slowly becoming a ruin.

The eyesore offended some residents, but it took a bird's-eye view to see the real potential of the place. Lenore Lee took one look from above and knew what she'd do with it. After months of repair and renovation, she announced the opening of Nevermore Books, Shady Hollow's very first bookstore.

The building's height was used to advantage. Every floor was dedicated to a different topic: fiction, history, philosophy, and more. Books lined the outer walls, while the center of the building was an atrium, so that browsing was like walking along a series of balconies. A creature could lean over the railing in the history section and see who was looking at the memoirs across the way.

The shop filled a niche in the town, and Lenore was kept quite busy.

Vera let out a heavy breath as she entered the bookshop. It was a soothing oasis, and at the moment it was relatively free of customers, since it was before the lunch hour, when some creatures of the town would take a browsing break from their workday.

Lenore had heard the bell over the door tinkle merrily, and she drifted down from the upper level where she had been conducting an inventory of the philosophy section. Lenore was a raven, you see, and her shop was set up so she could access all of the floors by wing. (There were stairs for flightless customers.)

Vera greeted her friend. "You'll never guess what turned up at the orchard this morning."

"I expect something besides a fruit tree." As Lenore had been working uninterrupted since dawn, she had no idea what had been occurring outside the sanctum of the bookstore.

"A body was dug up," Vera reported. "A skeleton, really. It must have been there for quite some time. Here's the oddest thing—it appears to be that of a very large creature. Dr. Broadhead guessed a moose."

"A moose? Oh, dear." Lenore looked surprised but only for a moment. Then she stared beyond Vera, lost in thought.

Vera nudged her friend. "What do you know?"

Vera had lived in Shady Hollow for a relatively short time, but Lenore had been there her whole life. And she read constantly, so there was almost nothing she didn't know when it came to village history.

Lenore spoke slowly, "I don't know anything for sure, but there was an incident . . . About fifteen or so years ago, a couple of moose came to town. Husband and wife. What a stir, especially when they opened a café—none other than Joe's Mug. They had a son shortly after. Things were grand for a while, but not long after Joe's Mug opened, Joe's wife disappeared. I think her name was Julia."

Vera desperately wanted to ask questions, but she knew Lenore wasn't finished with her story.

"No one really thought anything of it," the raven went on. "Julia wasn't particularly popular, and no one knew her that well. You have to understand that she was as aloof as Joe is gregarious. Then one day, she was gone. Joe didn't say much, but most of us assumed that Julia had left him and Joe Junior and that he didn't really want to talk about it. Who would?"

"But there was never a suggestion that she died?" Vera prompted.

"Oh, no." Lenore shook her feathered head. "Not a whisper. Joe and Julia bickered at the café—folks could see that theirs was a strained relationship. But as for what happened . . . she was a young, healthy creature. Why should anyone suspect anything bad had become of her?"

"What if something did happen to Julia?" Vera ventured to ask. "What if someone conked her on the head and buried her in the orchard? Joe would think that she'd left without a word, and he might've been too angry to find out for sure. No one else would have suspected anything other than that Julia had gotten tired of her family and headed for greener pastures."

"Don't get too carried away, Vera," Lenore cautioned. "You

said yourself it's only a guess so far. We don't even know for sure if that skeleton belongs to a moose, much less to a particular moose."

"It could be much older, too," Vera admitted. "I suppose moose bones might last a long time." The wheels were already turning in her active brain. Vera had a nose for news, and there was a story here. She was sure of it!

"I have to get back to work," Vera informed her friend. "Thanks for the information about Julia. I'm going to look into it."

"Just be careful," Lenore warned. "Who knows what we'll do if there is another murderer running amok in Shady Hollow. The town hasn't fully recovered from what happened last time."

"You don't know it's foul play. It's perfectly possible that some poor moose got sick and died in that spot and the earth slowly covered them up a hundred years ago!"

"We should be so lucky," Lenore muttered, displaying the traditional optimism of a raven.

Vera promised to be cautious and bade her friend goodbye. She needed to get to the newspaper office as soon as possible. She'd meant to check in hours ago, and after hearing Lenore's story, she was aching to do some research on the disappearance of Joe's wife. Vera's mind was whirling as she hurried to the Shady Hollow *Herald*. She hoped no one would want to talk to her. She didn't have time for idle chatter, at least not until she turned in her new article. As Vera reached the loud, busy main room of her place of employment, she said a silent prayer that all her colleagues were involved in their work and were not milling around looking for diversions. She breathed a sigh of relief as she scurried to her desk without having to speak to any coworkers, especially Gladys Honeysuckle. Vera was certain that Gladys would have heard about the grisly discovery at the orchard by now and would be looking for details to include in her next gossip column.

Vera put a fresh piece of paper in her typewriter and hit the keys furiously as she transcribed her written notes. Then she revised her words again, shortening the article and highlighting all the important points so her readers would know what happened.

When she was happy with the piece, she rushed it up to her editor's office.

The editor of the *Herald* was a skunk named BW Stone, and he ran the paper with an accountant's shrewd efficiency and an entertainer's eye for spectacle. Stone also smoked cigars morning, noon, and night, causing his office to be perpetually shrouded in a gray cloud.

"Got something for you, BW," Vera said, trying not to cough.

The portly creature grabbed the article and read it with one eyebrow raised.

"'Discovery . . . bones . . . agitation . . . moose . . . mystery . . . await details from authorities . . .'" He looked up. "Excellent! We can really string this out and have folks talking for weeks. I think we might dribble in some interest pieces. The rabbits' shock! The fear of eating apples! Who could the moose have been? Excellent!"

"Dr. Broadhead will have a report for Orville soon," Vera said. "I intend to go over to the police station and hear the results of his tests once he lets Orville know."

"Not so fast, Vixen." Stone pulled out a new cigar and looked at the unclipped end critically. "You've been so busy with bones in orchards that you wouldn't know that place on Elm has been rented, finally."

"I saw the movers this morning—" she began to say.

"Good! Your next assignment is to go there and find out what's coming in."

"But the orchard—"

"The bones have been buried there for years, Vera. This isn't exactly a hot lead. Do a story on the new business, whatever it is, and then you can dabble in bones again. Understand?"

"Sure thing, Boss." Vera waved a file folder like a fan to clear the smoke from her immediate vicinity. Though it irked her, she knew BW was right. The newspaper existed to serve all the residents of the town, and as a reporter she had to write stories on all kinds of goings-on in Shady Hollow. In any case, Orville wouldn't have the results from the tests until tomorrow at the earliest. So she might as well put the situation from this morning aside and follow Stone's instructions to interview the new business owner.

Vera returned to her desk to tidy up before heading back out to locate the mysterious new owner of the mysterious new business. There was a brisk tapping at the side of her desk, and she looked up to see Gladys Honeysuckle hovering near her.

"Have you heard the latest?" Gladys twittered, not waiting for Vera to greet her. "Bones in the orchard!"

"Yes," Vera said smoothly, "I just filed an article about it. It'll be in tomorrow's issue."

"You. Filed. An. Article." Gladys's eyes took on a different sort of sheen, one tinged with green. "A whole article?"

"I happened to be around when the news was announced. Lucky break." Vera gave a little shrug to show that it didn't really matter, but Gladys had already zoomed away. Well, the gossip columnist thought she had a scoop on Vera, who was a news reporter! Ha!

Still, she hadn't liked the look Gladys had given her. Hummingbirds generally are not known to be aggressive, but they generally aren't known to write scandal sheets, either. Vera would have to watch Gladys carefully to make sure the bird wasn't planning any kind of vengeance.

Then again, hummingbirds often move too fast to see.

Chapter 5

A little while later, Vera headed over to the formerly empty storefront on Elm Street to get the lay of the land. A new sign had been placed in the window; the words were written in a bold, elegant style.

"'Grey's School of Etiquette,'" Vera read out loud. "'Now enrolling.'" Fastened to the glass was a smaller sheet explaining that etiquette was an "essential art" and that students could sign up for classes in table manners, modes of address, formal dance, and more.

She knocked on the door, suddenly wondering if there was a proper way to knock.

No one answered, so she knocked again, louder this time. "Surely less polite," she told herself.

Still, the door remained closed and locked. Whoever or whatever Grey was, they were not coming to greet a caller.

The afternoon was wearing on, so it was possible that the new tenant had simply decided to close early. Or they'd peeked from a window and decided that Vera looked too much like a reporter—a reaction she was quite familiar with.

But reporters are tenacious, and Vera resolved to try again early the next morning. She stopped by the police station only to hear that nothing new had been discovered. Orville pointed to a stack of papers on his desk and said he'd be stuck there filing things till late. Vera took the hint and left him to his work.

She spent a quiet night at home, enjoying an old Bradley Marvel thriller while sipping peppermint tea. That is, she enjoyed the novel up until the scene where Marvel's hero discovered a cache of bones, which hinted at more dire revelations to come. Vera put the book down, staring at the leaping flames in her hearth. Life was not a novel, but she had a hunch that the bones in the orchard *also* hinted at more dire revelations to come.

After a night of restless sleep, Vera woke up ready to face another day, no matter what it might bring. She ate a bowl of oatmeal studded with cranberries and drank a large cup of strong tea to fortify herself against the sunny but brisk morning.

When Vera neared Grey's School of Etiquette, she noticed that the front door was propped open with a heavy stone block to let in the fresh air. *Excellent!* she thought, strolling inside. Vera found herself in an empty reception area. On one wall hung a large bulletin board posted with a calendar of events, so she moved in for a closer look, pushing her glasses up with one paw.

Something was going on at the school every day of the week except Sunday. Letter writing, elocution, and ballroom dancing seemed to be the main subjects. Vera was noting the times and dates in her little notebook when she heard steps behind her.

"May I help you?" asked a cool voice.

Vera whirled around to see an elegant mink observing her, waiting for an answer. All minks have a natural elegance because of their body shape and lovely coats. This mink, however, was in a class by herself.

Her coat was a gleaming soft silvery color, despite the fact that she could not be any older than Vera. She was also slender and stood unusually tall, with the sort of easy grace that made it difficult to look away. The mink's dark eyes were intent, raking over Vera as though searching out any speck of dust. Vera remembered then that her outfit really did need to be sent to the cleaners. She'd thought she'd get one more wear out of it first. Oops. She had never felt less prepared for an interview.

"Cat got your tongue?" the mink prompted. She was holding something in her right paw, and it took Vera a moment to recognize it as a copy of that day's edition of the *Herald*. The newspaper seemed far too ordinary for such a glamorous creature to possess.

Vera stuck out a paw and introduced herself. "Hello! I'm Vera Vixen, with the Shady Hollow *Herald*. I'd like to speak to you about your new business if you have a few moments."

"A reporter," the mink said with a slight edge of distaste in her cultured voice, "for the newspaper."

"Yes. And I'd love to hear about your business," Vera said with more enthusiasm than she felt.

The mink peered at Vera's still-outstretched paw but made no move to shake it. "I am Ms. Octavia Grey," she said. "I appreciate the interest, but I'm afraid that I am far too busy for an interview just now. So much to do with getting the business ready for our first customers, you see."

Vera slowly dropped her paw to her side. She did *not* see how Ms. Grey could possibly be that busy, as there was no one else here, but she nodded, feeling a little cowed by the silver mink.

"Perhaps another time?" she asked. "The *Herald* is widely read! I'll just leave you my card. Please contact me at your convenience." Vera placed her business card on the reception desk when Ms. Grey made no move to take it from her. Then she left without another word, feeling the mink's eyes on her until she was out of sight of the school.

What a strange creature, Vera thought. Ms. Grey certainly wasn't going to bring students in with her charm. How on earth could she teach etiquette and manners when she herself was so unwelcoming? Vera continued down the street and decided that it would be a cold day in hell before she set foot in that place again unless the mink changed her tune. This reporter had much bigger things to worry about than some stranger traipsing into town telling folks that she knew more about manners than the locals!

The police station was only a couple blocks outside Vera's route, so she detoured and stopped inside.

"Vera!" Orville looked up at her in surprise. "You're here early."

"Well, I thought I'd see if you've heard anything yet."

"Nope. Dr. Broadhead told me that he might have something around noon. Till then, I've got some other issues to deal with. Good article by the way."

"Thanks." Vera felt flattered. Orville always read the paper from cover to cover, but he rarely commented on any of the items. "Well, I'm off to work. Let me know if Broadhead's report has anything interesting in it."

At the *Herald*'s offices, Vera spent the morning looking through the newsroom's vertical files, which were kept on just about any creature or event in the town's history, no matter how obscure. Some folders, like "Lost Gazebo of Spring Pond," held only a few clippings—in this case, a flood had isolated and eventually taken down a once-beautiful structure. For other topics, multiple files were jam-packed with information.

Flipping past labels for Ash & Acorn Gifts and Bramblebriar Bed & Breakfast, Vera found the file for Cold Clay Orchards. She learned that it had been founded more than fifty years ago and had steadily expanded since its beginnings. She compared the map of the orchard property with old maps of the town. The land the orchard stood on had been wilderness until it was cultivated by the owners of Cold Clay. Vera hoped to find evidence that the place had once hosted a cemetery, which would explain the bones in a much less ominous way than what she feared was the case.

After a while, Vera turned to other topics. Joe's Mug rated a file, unsurprisingly. So did its owner, Joe Elkin. Vera laughed a little as she realized that she had never heard Joe's last name before. He was always just Joe to her and probably to most of the town. She went through the stack of papers in the file and caught sight of an article about a divorce decree that was dated approximately four years ago. The notice informed Vera that Joseph Oliver Elkin had been granted a divorce from Julia Iris Elkin on the grounds of abandonment. Mr. Elkin was granted full custody of Joseph Junior, the couple's only son. The court clerk noted that Julia's failure to appear in court and her unknown whereabouts meant Joe won the case by default. No other details were provided in the very short notice.

Vera sat back in her wooden chair to contemplate this information. Joe must have thought Julia had abandoned her family, and he wanted closure. Vera wondered if he'd tried to contact Julia before seeking the divorce. Had he heard anything from her at all? If so, it would disprove one possible explanation for the identity of the bones.

Vera put the files back just as her tummy rumbled. It was definitely lunchtime, and she hadn't packed a meal that morning.

When Vera arrived at Joe's Mug, the diner was full with the lunch crowd. Vera surveyed the room, watching various creatures in little groups, all with their heads together and whispering furiously. Some had copies of the paper on their tables. Joe, however, seemed to be exactly the same as always. He was his usual pleasant self, chatting with customers as he filled their orders for food and drinks. If he knew that the bones were suspected of belonging to a moose, he didn't let on.

As Vera waited her turn in line at the counter, she desperately tried to come up with some small talk. She had known this gentle creature for years, and now she was almost afraid to say anything for fear of upsetting him. She racked her brain for some inane comment about the weather or some harmless chatter from Gladys's latest gossip column. But then again, Joe usually knew the gossip before it was ever printed in the first place.

Before Vera reached Joe to place her order, the bell over the front door rang loudly as the door was pushed open with extra force. Vera turned to see Orville striding in. Her heart sped up as she realized that Orville must have heard some news about the bones, and he certainly hadn't told her before acting on it! The police bear was methodical and rarely jumped to conclusions, so his serious expression meant something . . . serious.

Vera frowned. The crowd at the front of the diner parted unconsciously as Orville advanced. They remained in earshot, however. No creature wanted to miss any drama in this town. Orville didn't look at anyone, not even Vera. He walked directly up to the counter, where the proprietor was standing with an expression of confusion on his face.

Orville tried to keep his voice down, but his words were audible to most of the nosy folks milling around the front of the shop.

"Well, Joe . . . er . . . Mr. Elkin," he announced succinctly, "I'm afraid I need to ask you to come to the station to answer some questions." At this, Joe's expression of confusion deepened. *Oh, no,* Vera thought. *He really has no idea what this is about.* Joe turned away from the police bear for a moment to whisper something to his son, Joe Junior, who was hovering nervously nearby. Joe Senior came around the counter and stood in front of Orville.

"How long do you think this will take?" he asked with almost no trace of alarm in his tone.

"Just come with me, Mr. Elkin," Orville replied formally. "I'll be the one asking the questions."

This is not going to help! Vera desperately wanted to intervene and say something, anything, to keep this from happening. She knew Orville would be furious if she interfered with official police work. So she literally bit her tongue to keep herself quiet as Joe walked slowly out of his own establishment, followed by Orville. The café was oddly silent as the customers watched them leave.

The door banged shut behind them, and the bell issued another indignant *ding*. Apart from that, the silence continued for a few seconds, and then the noise level rose significantly as every creature present began to chatter to their neighbor. Vera couldn't bear to hear the speculation, so she moved to leave as quickly as she could, lunch completely forgotten. Judging by Orville's demeanor and his forcible request to Joe, someone had discovered a link between the bones and the missing Julia Elkin. Things were not looking good for her large friend.

Chapter 6

Amid the hubbub in the café and as Vera was leaving, a stoat leaned over to the fox. "You going to write an article on *that?*"

"Count on it," Vera snapped, her hackles rising. Not only would she write an article about Orville forcibly bringing Joe in for questioning, she'd get some new information that would actually illuminate the situation for her readers.

But she couldn't just follow Orville to the station. That wouldn't do at all. Instead she would head back to the orchard, where it all began, and learn what she could at the scene itself. That was the first step. Once she got a clue there, she'd know where to go next.

When Vera arrived at Cold Clay Orchards, however, she felt

at a loss; she didn't know exactly what to look for. The apple-picking crew had moved on to the next row, leaving the area by the cordoned-off hole where the bones had been discovered very quiet.

By this point, the bones were gone. Orville had directed the unearthing of the remainder and had them all sent to Dr. Broadhead's office.

Vera padded around the perimeter of the hole, looking down into it but also out toward the surrounding fields and forest. What brought the creature here? What caused it to drop dead here? And most important, why had the body been buried at all? That meant someone had come upon the dead creature and chose to hide the body rather than tell anyone. Very strange indeed.

Out of the corner of her eye, Vera spied a young rabbit hovering nervously at the end of the row of trees. She was a little too young to be one of the pickers. She looked like she ought to be in school.

"Excuse me, Miss Vixen," said the newcomer. Ever since the summertime incident, every creature in town knew Vera's name, although Vera had no idea who this was.

"Yes," she said kindly; the rabbit seemed extremely nervous. "May I help you?"

"My name is Winifred. I've got something to show you."

Vera struggled to keep her expression neutral as she considered Winifred with interest. The rabbit looked toward the area where the apple pickers worked, then dangled something shiny from her paw. "Here."

Vera bent her head to take a closer look. It was a silver heart-shaped locket with a hinge on one side and a broken chain. Vera took the necklace in her own paw and released the catch that held the locket closed. Inside was a small photo of a moose, a young male with a rack of antlers that fit rather perfectly in the two lobes of the heart-shaped locket. He looked vaguely familiar.

Vera locked eyes with Winifred, who was watching her closely. "Odd sort of thing for a rabbit to be carrying around," Vera noted.

"Oh, it's not mine. I found it in the orchard."

"You were out here yesterday morning? Shouldn't you have been in school?"

Winifred said earnestly, "No, that's just the thing. I didn't find it yesterday, not in the . . . grave. I found it years ago, when I was little. It was summer then and really hot, even at night. That's why I wanted to go to the orchard early in the morning before it got any hotter. Anyway, the locket was lying in the grass below a tree. I noticed it only because it was sunny and the sun was shining right on it. When I was older, I realized that the summer I found the locket was the same summer when Julia Elkin disappeared."

"So you picked it up," Vera said. "Natural enough. Do you think the locket has anything to do with the grave, though? Someone could have lost it at any time."

Winifred gave a quick shake of her head, and her long ears flapped about. "I found it right near where the bones were uncovered. The *moose* bones." She nodded significantly toward the locket, which did strongly suggest a link to the moose.

"Tell me," Vera said, "did you ever meet Joe's wife?"

"No, but I remember when she left town. My mother and aunts went on about it when they thought we all were asleep. I was young, but I know it was the same summer I found this."

"I see."

"Please take that locket, Miss Vixen," Winifred urged. "Maybe it will help you find out what's going on here." The rabbit rushed on, glancing around again to make sure no one could overhear them. "Mr. Joe has always been so nice to me," she said, "and I don't want anything bad to happen to him. I know you'll find out about that body."

While Vera was flattered by Winifred's confidence in her abilities, she wasn't certain the locket would help Joe's cause. Despite the rather suspicious coincidence of this moose-adorned locket showing up near the grave, Vera felt certain that Joe was innocent of any wrongdoing. But how could she really know for sure, and how would it look to others?

Rather than reveal any of her inner turmoil to the young creature she had just met, Vera smiled and patted Winifred on the shoulder. "I appreciate your trust in me," she said slowly, "but why not take it to the police?"

"The police spend their time fishing," Winifred replied, a statement that was certainly true of half the police force, although it also implicated Orville by association. "What can they do? I know that you'll search for the truth."

Vera thanked the young rabbit again and took the locket as she said her goodbyes. She desperately wanted to delve into this case more, but how could she without upsetting Orville and the official police investigation?

On her way back to the *Herald* newsroom, Vera decided that, for the moment, she would keep her investigation to herself if at all possible. However, time was of the essence. Vera could foresee a future in which Joe was accused of a most heinous crime based on mere bones and a bit of speculation. He and his business would not survive if he were imprisoned. Joe Junior would never be able to keep the café going on his own.

And how long would it take before the young moose learned his mother had been murdered, perhaps by his own father? It didn't bear thinking about. Vera had to learn the truth before things went rapidly downhill.

At the thought of Joe's Mug, Vera changed her route. She could use a cup of coffee, after all, and the events of the day had prevented her from getting one earlier. The café was busy as usual, although there was a sense of chaos in the air that was certainly *not* usual. Joe Junior was in the kitchen, frantically running from the stove to the sink and back, trying to do three jobs at once. A few bar towels hung from his antlers.

Behind the counter stood Esmeralda von Beaverpelt in her crisp uniform: a striped dress and a starched white apron. No one would guess Esmeralda was once considered a snobby heiress. She wore a name tag that said ESME and had a pencil stuck behind one ear as she rang up a customer's bill.

"Ten eighty, Mr. Fallow. Exact change appreciated. Ah, thank you. And what a nice hat, sir. New? Very dashing." Even as Esmeralda took the money given to her by the rat, she called back over her shoulder, "Joe, how's it coming? I've got that order for table five. Four grillies and a basket of zucchini fries!"

"Coming up!" Joe shouted back. "New pot of coffee is ready!"

With a satisfied *hmm*, Esme spun around to grab the coffeepot by the handle with one paw and flip the counter up with another, and then she walked into the main dining area. "Who needs a refill?" she barked.

Several paws lifted mugs into the air, making it look like the creatures were all proposing a toast. Esme hurried around the café, pouring coffee as if she'd been doing it her whole life rather than just a few weeks.

The beaver maid spotted Vera just then. "Coffee, Miss Vixen?" she asked.

"Yes, indeed." Vera slid onto one of the stools at the counter and flipped over the mug that had been placed there. "Busy day."

"They're all busy," Esme replied, pouring the steamy rich brew into the mug, "but it's way tougher with the original Joe not here. I never realized all the stuff he did without ever thinking or talking about it! Hope he gets back soon."

"We all do, I'm sure," Vera said, knowing she spoke for the town. Everyone liked Joe. He was a fixture in Shady Hollow, always ready to offer a warm plate of food and listen to his customers with a kind ear. Folks shared good news and bad with Joe. But who did *he* confide in? Vera realized just how mysterious the gentle giant was.

"I wonder, Esme, if you think you could spare Joe Junior for a moment? I'd like to ask him something."

"Oh, not now, we're going to get a rush. How about after closing? Or when Joe gets back?"

"Sure, I'll come by after closing," Vera said. She hastily took a sip of coffee, mostly to avoid saying her fear—that it might be a while before Joe left the police station—out loud.

Esme bustled around, attending to more customers. Vera twisted in her counter seat, enjoying the coffee and looking over the outwardly normal scene. *Maybe I'm just borrowing trouble,* she thought. It was perfectly possible that Orville had already asked Joe some general questions and then sent him on his way. The deputy tended to get overly formal in new situations—Vera remembered that aspect of their very first date, when he'd held all the doors for her and pulled out her chair to be seated at dinner. Vera was all for equality, but it was awfully nice to know that chivalry still existed in the world. She was sure that, no matter the situation, Orville would treat Joe with the same courtesy he showed everyone.

In fact, she ought to go to the police station just to prove it. She was a reporter, after all. She would report what she discovered and have a tidy little column about Orville's policing techniques. That would be what BW called a feel-good piece, not to mention that Orville might be more apt to share details of his investigation with her after a flattering article appeared.

"Hey, Esme, box up a couple slices of apple pie for me, would you?" Vera called out. She had an idea.

Moments later, a white paper box was deposited on the counter, with a red-inked apple drawn on the top in Esme's bold style. Draining the last of the coffee in her mug, Vera dropped a bill on the counter and gathered her things. She slipped a paw into her bag, feeling the heavy locket nestled there. She really ought to tell Orville about it. It could be evidence.

"Then again, it was found a *long* time ago," she muttered to herself as she walked down the street. "It's not as if it's a murder weapon or something like that!" Justifying her failure to share information with Orville made Vera a little squirmy—it was one thing to be sly, and quite another to be dishonest—but she could always show it to him later. "I'll just see what's what first."

The police station was in a handsome stone building farther down Main Street, and it didn't take Vera long to reach the front door. Burdened with the pie box, she pushed it open with her back, already hearing voices raised in a heated exchange.

"Just answer the question, sir!" That was Orville; he sounded frustrated.

"I *can't*. I don't remember. That's the only answer I can give." Joe's voice was a lower pitch and a tad calmer, though he, too, was clearly running out of patience.

Vera saw them sitting on opposite sides of Orville's large wooden desk. Both appeared rather worn out, which was understandable if the questioning had gone on for so long. Then again, Joe wasn't behind bars in one of the cells, so that was a positive sign.

"Excuse me," she said, stepping fully into the room. "Am I interrupting?"

Vera wasn't above a well-timed bat of the eyelashes, and Orville seemed momentarily speechless when he looked at her.

"Uh . . . no, Miss Vixen. Well, that is, I'm in the middle of an interrogation . . ." He trailed off when Vera held up the box from the diner. The smell of cinnamon and cloves wafted into the air. "Is that pie?" Orville asked.

"One for you and one for Joe," Vera said cheerfully. "I imagine you've both had a long day and could use a treat."

Pie makes for an effective truce, and soon both the police bear and his witness were devouring their slices.

"Mmmm, good stuff," Orville said between bites.

"Not bad," Joe commented professionally. "Tastes like Joe Junior might have added a dash too much sugar in this batch. Or the apples weren't as tart."

"How do you know it was his batch and not yours?" Vera asked, genuinely curious about the answer.

Joe gently tapped the flaky golden crust with his fork. "The pinpricks in the crust. He always does a different pattern than I do."

"My goodness." Vera had never noticed the pinprick patterns before, and she had eaten *plenty* of pie from Joe's Mug since moving to town. "Well, I expect you'll be back in the kitchen soon and putting your own pattern on the next batch."

"That's up to the deputy," Joe said quietly.

Vera looked over to Orville, whose face was half covered by his plate. He'd been licking the last of the apple filling.

Orville put the plate down hastily. "Um, right. Procedure, you know. I've got to ask all the questions."

"And if the answer is 'I don't remember,' what do you do next?" Vera raised an eyebrow. "Joe's been here for hours. He must have told you what he knows by now."

Orville frowned but didn't reply.

"And if you think of new questions," Vera added in her most reasonable tone, "you always know where to find Joe. He's going to be at work. Joe Junior and Esme can't wait to see him back. Not to mention all the customers!"

"I suppose so," Orville said slowly. "All right, Joe, you can go. But I'll have more questions for you later."

"Come on down to the café and ask, then," Joe said, lumbering up to his full height, which was quite impressive. He walked out of the station, leaving Vera and Orville alone.

Vera glanced about, noting the empty chair behind Chief Meade's desk. "The chief is out again, I see."

"Trout are running," Orville said in explanation. "Probably the last big run before the cold sets in." In most cases, the chief's vice wasn't an issue since Orville preferred to do his policing without interference. Now he looked at Vera with narrowed eyes; he was very much in his role as deputy. "Why do you ask? Are you here as a member of the press, as a friend to Joe, or as a friend to me?"

"Why do I have to choose?" Vera countered. "It won't change the answers to my questions, will it? Come on, Orville. You can't honestly believe Joe had anything to do with the bones buried in the orchard. He's not the type to do something under cover of darkness . . . or whenever those bones were buried."

"I've lived here a lot longer than you, fox," Orville reminded her.

"And in all that time have you ever seen Joe do something violent?"

"No," Orville said slowly, "but I do remember when his wife disappeared. He acted funny for weeks afterward."

"Maybe he acted funny because *his wife left him.*" Vera rolled her eyes. "Folk handle rejection in different ways, you know. Their reaction doesn't prove anything. And honestly, we still don't even know if the body belongs to Julia. Do we?"

"Not for certain," Orville admitted. "Dr. Broadhead's preliminary work suggested it's a female moose, though, due to the size of the femurs and the absence of antlers."

"So it could be some other moose. Maybe not even a resident of the Hollow." As Vera spoke, she suddenly remembered the locket in her bag. If Vera could confirm that Julia once wore that locket, it would go a long way toward proving the bones *were* hers.

"I've got to do something," Orville said, sounding unhappy. "I can't allow bones to be discovered and then just stand around. Folk want action."

"Investigation is action," said Vera. "That's what *I'm* doing."

"What do you mean when you say you're investigating?"

"Oh! I just meant that I'm going to write a story about it. Can I get a quote from you, Deputy?" She whipped out her notebook and put on her interested-reporter expression, though Orville still looked skeptical.

"What do you want me to say?" Orville growled. "I'm investigating. The scene is off-limits until further notice. And folks have nothing to worry about. There's no reason to think anyone is in danger today. Whoever it was, that body was buried years ago."

Vera scribbled it all down. "Thanks! Well, got to dash!"

"I thought maybe you'd want to have dinner tonight?" Orville asked then, in a much different tone.

Oh, no! She had already made plans to meet up with Joe Junior after the café closed. "Um, I think we'll both be too busy working. Maybe tomorrow?"

"All right then." Orville nodded, looking a little sad.

Vera left the police station, feeling bad about canceling their almost date. But it was true—they both had work to do.

Chapter 7

Vera trotted back to the offices of the *Herald*, feeling as if she would soon wear a groove in the sidewalk between the police station and her place of employment. Good thing Shady Hollow was a small town! When she arrived, there was a note on her desk asking her to see BW when she returned. Vera sighed. Most of her interactions with the skunk involved her standing in the doorway of his paper-packed office while he barked orders and puffed on an enormous cigar. Vera always knew it had been a particularly difficult day when she could smell smoke in her fur long after returning home in the evening.

Talking with BW was the sort of task that got more onerous when put off, so Vera took a few deep breaths and then walked to his office.

"What's up, Boss?" she asked, tapping lightly on the open door.

"Please come in, Miss Vixen," crooned the skunk. Vera was startled. Stone usually just called her "Vixen." Or "Vera." Or "fox"—or nothing at all, depending on his mood. Yet now he was unusually and alarmingly cheerful. Vera had never seen him this way.

"I heard from that Octavia Grey creature," BW said as soon as Vera was inside his office. "A very charming mink. You did contact her, didn't you?"

"Um, yes. Briefly," Vera started to explain. "She was busy at the time, but I left a card—"

"Oh, you get your tail right back there, Vera. She wants to run an ad in the paper. A *big* ad."

Vera understood immediately why her boss was in such a good mood. The only thing Stone liked more than a big newsworthy scandal was money. And big ads meant big money, at least for the paper. Not many of the local businesses bothered advertising in the *Herald*, mostly because everyone knew about them already. However, Grey was opening a new business . . . something that had not happened in Shady Hollow for quite a while.

In her reflective moments, Vera often wondered about the future of the newspaper and her job. Not just the Shady Hollow *Herald*, but newspapers everywhere. So many creatures did not even bother reading papers, especially young ones. But Vera loved the paper. The thrill of getting a scoop. The peril of a deadline. The rumbling of the presses and the smell of ink! There was nothing better!

Vera shook herself out of her daydream. She realized her boss was staring at her expectantly. Apparently he'd been talking the whole time Vera had been reflecting on the future of journalism. Oops.

"I'm s-sorry, BW," she stammered. "Could you repeat that? I guess I'm still a little shaken up about the discovery at the orchard."

"What?" he barked. "Oh, right, the bones at the orchard. Nothing to worry about there. Old case. No news." He continued, "The big thing is that Octavia Grey wants to run a full-page ad with us announcing the opening of some kind of school."

"Her school of etiquette."

"Right, exactly. A full-page ad!"

Vera couldn't believe that Stone didn't think the discovery of a body in the orchard, no matter how old, was a story. She was itching to investigate it and not just to exonerate her friend Joe. Shady Hollow was Vera's home, and her neighbors were her community. She wanted to believe, had to believe, that the town was a safe place—barring a few recent incidents—and that her friends were innocent of wrongdoing.

"Here's where you come in, fox," continued the skunk, who was now pacing back and forth behind his desk, his fluffy tail following him like an attentive assistant. "I want you to get busy on that interview with Grey. Not a short piece, either, but a full profile. Get whatever you can out of her, and we'll run it on the front of the Features section with the ad on the next page."

"Sure thing, BW," Vera agreed, mostly to get him out of her path. "I'll get right on it."

"You do that, Vixen. I want it ASAP. Everything in black and white!"

As Vera returned to her desk and took care of the menial daily tasks that plague all reporters, she thought that Octavia must have been much more polite to BW Stone than she was when Vera visited the etiquette school. Maybe Octavia was one of those females who only comes to life when there's a male around. Vera found such creatures ridiculous, but they were everywhere. It made her head hurt.

By then, it was almost quitting time, so Vera decided to head home for a short while before she went to visit Joe Junior at the diner. It closed at eight o'clock in the evenings since it opened so early in the mornings. That meant Vera had a few hours to herself. She wanted to relax a bit, check her mail, and put her initial ideas about the bones in the orchard into some coherent notes. The interview with Octavia Grey dropped right out of her head. Vera had priorities, and the new mink's business venture wasn't one of them.

Vera lived in a neat, low-roofed, den-like cottage on a quiet street near the forest. She felt a surge of pride every time she saw her den. She had bought it herself with money she had saved, and she was very proud of that fact. She loved being independent and hoped that it would always be that way. Her cottage was very much a fox's home, though. Not a bear's.

Her mood soured a bit. As much as she was enjoying her nascent romance with Orville, she had no desire to have him take care of her while she puttered away at home, embroidering cushions or making doilies or doing whatever hobby was trendy. She was a journalist first and foremost, and any partner in her life would have to understand that. She and Orville weren't that serious yet, but she was fairly certain that he liked the fact that she had a career. Her career was the reason they met, after all. She knew that police work was important to Orville as well. They were an excellent match. But eventually would she be expected to give up her wonderful little Vera-sized home?

Once inside, she pushed off all the worries about her future—so far away!—and got to work on her notes. In due course, the clock edged toward the time when she ought to leave for Joe's Mug. Since it was well into autumn now, the sky was quite dark—except for the hundreds of stars sparkling overhead.

Vera inhaled the smells of woodsmoke and warm food as she walked by the homes of the Hollow's residents. There was the raucous Chitters household—two adult mice and uncountable children—all gathering around for Mrs. Chitters's famous cheese soup, best served with lots of bread for dipping.

Then she passed the home of several rabbits who worked at the *Herald* and roomed together to save costs (the newspaper was not the most lucrative employer). Vera sniffed and knew that roasted carrots and parsnips and, of course, green salad were on the menu tonight. One cannot stop a rabbit when it comes to salad.

As she walked on, the buttery, rich smell of walnut strudel nearly stopped her in her tracks. She didn't know Mr. Unterwald, a badger, very well—just enough to nod to in the street. But if walnut strudel appeared on his menu often . . . well, perhaps she ought to make an effort to chat with her neighbors more.

Vera's stomach was grumbling when she pushed open the door to Joe's.

"Sorry," Esme called out, looking up from the table she'd

been wiping clean, "we're closed . . . Oh, it's you, Vera. You want to talk to a Joe? They're both here." She sounded quite relieved about that last fact.

"I can wait till the closing tasks are done." Vera caught sight of a slice of pie under a glass dome, and her stomach growled again.

"Goodness. You want something to eat?" Esme asked.

Vera gave an embarrassed smile. She didn't think others could hear her tummy rumble! "I'll be all right."

"We've got some leek-and-onion stew that we can't keep overnight. If you don't eat it, I'll just have to toss it out."

"I *love* leek-and-onion stew," Vera admitted.

Esme walked into the kitchen, but it was Joe who brought out the tray a moment later, laden with a bowl of steaming stew and a couple dinner rolls. And, of course, a mug of coffee.

"Mmmm, thanks," Vera said. "I feel like I'm getting in the way of your cleaning, though, making more dishes."

"No trouble," Joe said. "Anyway, if you hadn't bribed the deputy this afternoon, I might still be stuck in that station."

"Bribed?" Vera asked, widening her eyes.

The moose winked at her. "Oh, you may call it apple pie, but I know a bribe when I see one."

"Then I must have been bribing you, too, since I gave you a slice."

"Perhaps you were, Vera. You're going to ask me some questions of your own, aren't you?"

"True." Vera put down her spoon. "Before that, though, I have something to show you, and it might not be very pleasant."

"That's in keeping with the rest of my day." Joe sighed— a moose sighing was certainly a sight to see.

Vera slapped a paw onto her napkin to keep it from blowing away with the force of Joe's sigh. Then she reached into her bag. She withdrew the locket on its chain.

"Does this look familiar to you?" she asked gently. By the expression on Joe's face, she already knew the answer.

The big creature reached out and just tapped the silvery locket, which sent it spinning around and catching the light from the café's kitchen. "Oh," he said. "Yes. I'd know that anywhere."

"That's Mother's!" another voice shouted.

Both Vera and Joe turned their heads to see Joe Junior standing by the counter. The young moose looked very upset. "Where'd you get that?" he demanded of Vera.

"One of the orchard workers found it and gave it to me earlier today."

"Found it with the body, you mean?" the elder Joe asked. A huge tear appeared in the corner of one of his eyes. "Then there's no hope, is there? It has to be Julia. I keep telling myself it has to be a stranger—"

Vera shook her head quickly. "We can't conclude anything yet. The locket was found in the orchard years ago—the same summer Julia left. But it's just possible that the two aren't linked."

"Of course they are," Joe Junior snapped, as angered as his father was sad. "Dad might want to believe she's alive still, but I know better. If Mother was alive, she would have come back home!"

"Calm down," Joe told his son.

"Why should I? It's been eleven years since she walked out, and today we find out she never even got past the town limits. It's not fair!"

With that, Joe Junior stormed through the kitchen and out of the café. The back door slammed.

Esme looked extremely uncomfortable at having been witness to Joe Junior's outburst. "Er, I guess I should go? Sorry . . . about everything. See you tomorrow for the breakfast shift."

"Good night, Esme," Joe said. "Be careful walking home."

Esme merely nodded as she let herself out the front door. Though the beaver showed little outward emotion, Vera was reminded that it had not been long since Esme had lost a parent—her father, Reginald, was murdered in late summer, his body found at the edge of the millpond. The news of the bones must have been very hard on everyone working at Joe's Mug, though each for different reasons. Yet Esme had worked all day long without fuss or complaint.

"Good help is hard to find," Joe said, nodding toward the departed waitress. "I should give her a raise. And you should eat that stew before it gets cold."

Knowing good sense when she heard it, Vera polished off the stew before resuming her questioning. After she got the last bit of stew by dragging a piece of roll across the bottom of the bowl, she said, "This must be a bad time for all of you. If you prefer, I could come back after this has all died down . . . that is, calmed down . . ."

Joe shook his massive head. "There's no good time to talk about this sort of thing, and I don't want to keep thinking about the past, so maybe telling you will help. You weren't living here when Julia left me, so you never met her."

"True," Vera agreed. As a relative newcomer to Shady Hollow, there were layers of knowledge about the community that she was still discovering. One thing she knew for certain, though, was that death always hastened the exposure of those layers. "Please tell me."

Joe paused before beginning the tale; perhaps he was anxious to tell it correctly the first time. "Like you, I didn't live in Shady Hollow when I was young. I grew up not too far away—just up north closer to the big mountains. I was happy enough, I suppose, though I always wanted to try something different. Even when I was young, I liked to cook and try out recipes. Got some ribbing from the family because of that—moose aren't known for their cooking. They sure thought it was funny that I was always in the kitchen. But they ate everything right up. My cloudberry custard pie was something, I tell you. I won all the pie contests. Secret is to drain the juices before baking—otherwise you get runny custard and a soggy crust."

Vera had no idea what a cloudberry even was, but she believed that any pie Joe made would be delicious. "Sounds like you had a calling."

"I did. And I guess I assumed Julia understood that, too. I met her when we were both young and restless, eager to explore the world and try new things. She was sweet and fun and always ready for an adventure. Marriage was an adventure." He nodded toward the locket. "I got her that as a wedding present. The picture is of me. Quite handsome I was back then!" he added wryly. Joe knew he wasn't a looker.

"It's a lovely piece of jewelry," Vera said. "She must have worn it every day."

"She did, from our wedding day until the last day I saw her." Joe sniffed as emotion suddenly overcame him.

"I gather you moved to Shady Hollow not long after your wedding," Vera said, hoping to help him focus.

"We did. We were happy here at first. I opened the diner pretty soon after, and I was ecstatic when customers actually showed up. Julia helped out behind the counter, and I thought she was happy, too."

"What changed?" Vera asked.

"The biggest change was Joe Junior. Julia stayed at home with him for a bit, and the diner got busier than ever, and I guess that was the beginning, even though I didn't know it then."

"Beginning of what?"

"Julia's restlessness. She'd always wanted adventure, and our life—café, child, home—just wasn't much of an adventure to her anymore. Early in our relationship, we'd talked about traveling across the continent, and it sounded grand but also sort of like a dream to me. She kept talking about places she wanted to go, things she wanted to do. None of them were around here, and none of them included me or our son."

Joe frowned and went on, "I tried to keep her happy. I bought her books about the places she mentioned, but looking at pictures instead of seeing them for herself only made her more frustrated. I spent more and more time at the café. We started to bicker every night. It made little Joe cry." Joe sighed again. "I should have tried harder."

"Did you try to stop her from leaving?"

"I didn't even know she intended to go!" Joe said. "She barely spoke to me those last couple months of our marriage. She was out of the house a lot, sometimes working at the café, but also with one or two of her friends who must have told her to leave the marriage."

"Who was that?"

"Honestly, I don't remember. Julia didn't have many friends, but I don't think I ever met them. She had her little circle at the end, and I had mine. It doesn't matter now, does it? Julia decided to leave, and no one was going to stop her. One night I got home from the café very late, and I heard Joe Junior crying in his bed. He'd had a nightmare. I went to him and called out for Julia—what parent lets their child cry like that?—and there was no response. She wasn't in the house. She'd left without a word. Not a note. Nothing."

"I'm so sorry, Joe." Vera put her paw out across the table. "And I'm sorry to have to ask, but do you happen to remember the date?"

"How could I forget? August third."

"And you never heard anything from her at all? Did you write to her family up north?"

"I did," Joe confirmed. "Hers and mine. I hoped she just went to her folks' home to teach me a lesson and that her family would let her know I wanted her to come back. But they hadn't seen her or heard from her. So I assumed that she really did what she said she was going to do: Travel. See the world. Wander. I hoped she was happy, wherever she was. It never occurred to me that—" Joe made a choking sound as he tried to stop a sob. "Excuse me, Vera. I've got to take care of some things. And find Joe Junior . . ."

"I understand," Vera said. "Forgive me for bothering you. Here, take the locket."

Joe stared at it dangling from Vera's paw. "No . . . not yet. Keep it for me, would you? I can't help but think that it will be bad luck for me to take anything of Julia's now."

"All right, Joe. I'll keep it safe." Vera put it in her bag again and then hurried out of the café, leaving Joe alone with the past.

Chapter 8

The next morning dawned beautiful and sunny. It was the perfect day for a fox to follow her nose and investigate a body that had recently turned up in the local orchard. Unless, of course, that same fox was gainfully employed by the local newspaper and owed her boss a story on the newest town resident and her business. Vera had little interest in Octavia Grey personally, but she *had* promised BW Stone an exclusive interview with the mysterious mink.

Using one of the town's courier squirrels—they ran around bearing everything from messages to meals—Vera had sent a note to Grey with a formal request for an interview and had received a surprisingly courteous and quick response indicat-

ing a date (today) and a time (half past nine) that were acceptable to Ms. Grey and her incredibly busy schedule. Much as
Vera would have loved to spend her day some other way, she
had to keep the appointment.

She made herself a simple breakfast of tea and toast, thinking that she didn't want to return to the diner and accidentally
upset Joe and his son any more than she already had. It was
a shame that all those feelings of loss had to be dragged into
the open again, but Vera intended to get to the bottom of the
situation as soon as possible. Or as soon as she wrote this silly
interview piece about Octavia.

Armed with her notebook, Vera set off for Elm Street and
Grey's School of Etiquette. She promised herself that she
would maintain her professional demeanor no matter how
condescending or rude the mink was. She and the creature
did not have to become dear friends, after all; this was simply Vera's job. When Vera reached the building, she knocked
sharply on the door, steeling herself for the worst.

Octavia answered the door immediately and greeted her
cordially.

"Good morning, Miss Vixen," purred the mink. "Won't you
please come inside? We can talk in my private office, where
we won't be disturbed. May I offer you tea or perhaps a café
au lait?"

Vera blinked in the face of all this effusive charm and racked
her brain to remember if there had been any mention of a second mink in town. This could not possibly be the same creature who had shut her down yesterday. Vera gathered herself
enough to request a café au lait.

"Very good. I'll be back in two shakes . . ." Octavia paused, then said, "I'm so glad you returned today. Yesterday I fear I was quite short with you, which is inexcusable for any creature but doubly so for someone in my position. Please accept my sincere apologies."

"Oh. Sure," Vera said, flustered. "Don't think anything of it. Believe me, I've heard worse."

"Well, I'll just get the drinks, then. Please have a seat."

Octavia left, and Vera settled herself in a richly upholstered wing chair in Octavia's fancy office.

She looked around in wonder. The office was beautifully furnished with dark mahogany pieces and colorful ornate rugs. *The etiquette business must be booming,* Vera thought as she took in her surroundings. She could hear the faint hissing of steam as Octavia prepared coffee for her guest. And that was how Vera felt at the moment: as if she were an honored guest in someone's home and not a reporter here for a story. Oddly, the feeling didn't sit well with her. She didn't want to like Octavia after yesterday.

Before Vera could begin to add up the cost of everything in Octavia's office, the mink returned with two porcelain cups and saucers on a silver tray. Inviting foam topped each beverage and there was an intoxicating aroma of rich coffee in the air. On a small table near Vera's chair, Octavia placed one cup, a small silver spoon, and a tiny silver dish filled with sugar cubes and a small pair of tongs.

Against all her instincts, Vera was enchanted. She put a tiny cube of sugar in her coffee and stirred it delicately while searching her brain for an opening question. So disarmed was Vera by how pleasantly she was being treated that her usual litany of interview questions had quite deserted her.

Octavia, who was either unaware of Vera's discomfort or too polite to comment on it, seated herself behind her desk—a delicate affair with intricately carved legs. She sipped her coffee and looked attentively at the fox opposite her.

"Rote interviews can be so awkward, can't they?" she said at last. "Why don't I begin with my own story? I expect you are wondering just how I ended up in your charming town."

The mink leaned back slightly in her chair—her posture was exquisite—and began to speak about her early life. Vera had collected herself enough to take out her notebook and pencil. She listened to Octavia's well-modulated voice and was fairly certain that this story had been rehearsed and told many, many times before.

"The Greys, you know, are a very old and well-regarded family," Octavia was saying. "My ancestors are blue-blooded minks who originally came from the Carbonia Mountains. There are long lines of aristocrats across the continent who bear the Grey surname in their histories. Fortunately the family has the financial means to support our illustrious background, and I am happy to say that I have been able to pursue my own interests without being forced to seek employment simply to make ends meet . . . not that I disdain work, of course. Work is so meaningful, is it not? You're a journalist, Miss Vixen. A very noble calling, indeed."

Flattery, Vera thought, even as she scribbled notes. And yet it felt rather good to be told one had a noble calling!

"I have heard," Octavia went on, "that you are a journalist of some tenacity. Some of the residents who welcomed me here told me all the latest news. You solved not one but two murders all by yourself! My goodness."

"Oh, I definitely had help from my friends," Vera mumbled, grateful that her blush could not be seen beneath her already-red fur.

"Intelligent *and* humble," Octavia said with an approving nod. "Very admirable. You are an example for today's youth. Just as I hope to be, in my own small way." She arced one limb outward to encompass the office and the school. "You understand that, due to my own upbringing, I have a wealth of knowledge on the matters of etiquette and good taste. When one meets royalty on a regular basis, one must be well prepared! And yet it seemed to me that knowledge on its own does very little. So I got the notion that I could share my knowledge with the populace."

Again the mink waved a paw. "I'm very excited. My new building is large, and there are several connecting rooms—so useful for classes. I'll have a course in ballroom dancing now that I have the space. This is a skill that most creatures don't possess, and opportunities to learn are few."

"You plan to place an advertisement for your school in the local paper," Vera noted.

"Indeed, although I have found that word of mouth is usually the best plan for gaining pupils. Wives will probably sign up for ballroom dancing—and register their husbands, too. It will get them out of the house one night a week."

"A date."

"Precisely. This facility also has a kitchen, which is essential. It's quite a challenge to teach proper table manners without any food. I plan to hire someone to prepare simple meals so that my students can practice their newly learned manners."

"You're an expert in all these subjects?" Vera asked, feeling a bit skeptical that one creature could be so refined. And yet, Ms. Grey did exude charm.

"One must be skilled at something!" Ms. Grey said with a laugh. "Through classes on etiquette and manners and dancing, I help other creatures to live in a more gracious and refined way. And that helps us all, does it not? A town is a better place when everyone is well mannered."

"What led you to choose Shady Hollow in particular?" Vera asked, secretly wondering if there were rumors circulating in the larger woodland that Shady Hollow was some kind of hotbed of rudeness. In fact, barring the occasional murder, Shady Hollow was as kind and friendly a town as any Vera had lived in.

"Oh, I just get a feeling about a place, you know," Octavia answered airily. "Something tells me Shady Hollow will be a wonderful beginning. Such a lovely and charming village. I can see folks' interest in life and their eagerness to better themselves. Just imagine—in addition to spelling bees, why not hold an etiquette bee? The contestants will prove their knowledge of proper behavior. Or a dance competition . . . Do you dance, Miss Vixen?"

"Only the foxtrot," Vera said. Dancing was not something she had much time for.

"You must come to a waltz class, then," Octavia said warmly. "What a pity that there are so few opportunities to indulge in a pleasurable pastime such as dancing. If you have a beau, you can bring him along."

Vera almost choked on the last of her drink. The idea of Orville on a dance floor was so foreign, she couldn't even picture it. "Maybe. One day."

Then she quickly asked one of her prepared questions, hoping to get the interview back on track.

Octavia replied, giving some account of her passion for teaching. Vera wrote it all down, thinking that this was far more background information than she had expected from Ms. Grey. In fact, Vera was now actually growing interested in the etiquette school and Octavia's plans for it. She almost didn't want the interview to end. The café au lait had been quite delicious, and the wing chair was extremely comfortable.

The calm was broken by a sharp knocking on the outer door of the school. Octavia looked startled, saying she wasn't expecting another caller, but excused herself to answer the door.

When the mink returned to her office, she was followed by an overdressed beaver who was similar to Esme in looks but very different in temperament.

"Why, Miss von Beaverpelt," said Vera, surprised. "What are you doing here?" Octavia's expression suggested that she was wondering the same thing.

Anastasia von Beaverpelt looked disdainfully at the fox. "Not that it's any of your business, Vera," she said shortly, "but I was interested in the etiquette school. I wanted to see how things are being done." She looked at the many ruffles on her skirt and fluffed out a few.

It suddenly dawned on Vera that the beaver might be in the market for a job. After all, her hardworking sister was contributing to the family's finances by waitressing at Joe's Mug. Working at the diner seemed like far too menial a job for a creature like Stasia, so perhaps she was seeking employment with Octavia. How interesting!

"Are you looking to become an assistant here?" Vera asked bluntly.

One look at Octavia told Vera that the business owner had come to the same conclusion.

"Assistant?" Anastasia's eyes widened in horror. "I don't assist anyone! I meant that I wanted to know if things are being done *properly*. Some creatures think they've got class, but they're just fooling themselves!" she announced, apparently without a wisp of self-awareness.

"Ah, of course," Octavia said, her voice smooth and controlled. "I understand your concern, Miss . . . von Beaverpelt, is it? I am Octavia Grey, the administrator of the school. You simply must join us for a class or two—with my compliments, bien sûr. I should be most interested to hear how my methods comport with your experience."

Anastasia narrowed her eyes and took a few moments to parse the response. She seemed to arrive at a conclusion she liked, because she finally nodded. "I *shall*."

"Very good. It was so kind of you to stop by," Octavia said, ushering the young beaver back out the way she had come. "I would speak more, but as you can see, I am in the middle of an interview with Miss Vixen. When the school opens officially, we must chat again. *Au revoir!*"

Once Anastasia was safely on the other side of the door, Octavia gave a little sigh and returned to her desk.

"I have to say," Vera confided, "you are your best advertisement. You handled Stasia better than anyone I've seen. She can be, er, challenging."

"A challenge has never scared me," Octavia replied with a little smile, "although I doubt she'll ever become an assistant here!"

"Are you hoping to hire one?" Vera asked.

Octavia shook her head gently. "Not at this time. I do feel it's vital to be the voice of the school. Later, though . . . perhaps. This is not the first venture I've founded, and it won't be the last. The whole world can benefit from teachings like mine, and I suppose I grow restless after a while."

Vera's pencil nib broke as she jammed it too hard into the paper. "Did you say *restless*?"

"Yes, darling. Does that surprise you? Some creatures have a nesting instinct, and some have wanderlust. I am the latter, for better or worse. Why? You look a little troubled."

"Ah, don't mind me. I've just heard that word rather a lot lately." Actually Vera had heard it only a few times, but since those times were in reference to Julia Elkin, the phrase echoed in disturbing ways. Vera shook her head once. "My goodness, look at the time. I have to get this story written, and you have to open a school! I'll be on my way."

"Thank you for stopping by, Vera—may I call you Vera? Ah, wonderful. You are welcome back anytime, of course. Good day!"

Chapter 9

Vera rushed to the newspaper office to write up her interview with Octavia Grey. Around her, dozens of creatures ran to and fro. Reporters barked out orders and requests to their assistants or, indeed, to any breathing creature who happened to be in range.

"Grab me that index on the Hollow's property transfers!" an old hare called.

"Does someone here know if aubergine is darker than burgundy?" The question came from the young otter who wrote the fashion column.

"If anyone uses the words *sting* or *stung* in articles about the spelling bee, BW says your pay will be docked! Remember, readers don't deserve clichés." That came from one of the senior reporters, Barry Greenfield, an older gray rabbit with a lot of white in his coat. "Detail, quote, punch, repeat! That's how to do it!"

"Detail, quote, punch, repeat," Vera's neighbor muttered under his breath, sounding as if he'd heard this advice for years. "We *know*, Barry."

Vera smiled to herself. For her part, she loved the din and the chaos of the newspaper office. All the bustle meant that folk cared. And every day, a new edition of the *Herald* meant that the whole town and the surrounding countryside would know what was happening.

Some creatures carried files or notes from one desk to another. Several writers pounded on typewriter keys until the cacophony of clacking noises made everyone have to yell. Two rabbits tossed headline ideas at each other so fast that the words could scarcely be discerned. Vera just hoped the resulting headlines would make sense.

Vera typed up her own notes as quickly as possible, eager to hit the deadline. When she finished, she yanked the last page from the typewriter and walked the article over to BW's office. The skunk had told her he wanted to edit the piece personally, which was another hint that Grey was going to be a very important client, spending quite a bit of money on ads and such.

"Excellent!" BW cried out when he saw the pages in Vera's grasp. He nearly spat out his cigar in his excitement. "I'll just spruce it up a bit, fox. You can get on to your next piece, whatever it is."

Vera was about to explain that she intended to write about the body in the orchard, which was now definitely identified as

Julia, but then saw that BW was already poring over the text of her article and completely oblivious to anything else.

"Okay, I'll talk to you later, BW," she said as she left the office.

The skunk didn't even reply.

When Vera stepped outside the newspaper office, she decided that she ought to see how Lenore was faring. The bookshop was only a few blocks away, and she wanted a breath of air.

In the bookshop, a few customers browsed the offerings. Lenore was keeping an eye on the whole place from her office perch on the top level. Vera waved from the ground floor, and Lenore glided down the open center of the store to land softly next to her.

"What's going on?" Lenore asked. "You look like you've got news."

"A few odds and ends," Vera said. She had meant to discuss the issue of the body and the very likely conclusion that it belonged to Julia Elkin. But for some reason the first thing that she said was "I talked to Ms. Grey this morning. The new mink."

"So you're the lucky one who gets to do a hard-hitting piece on the new etiquette school?" Lenore's humor was often drier than most folk were used to.

"It was an interview," Vera said, feeling a little hurt. "The residents should have a chance to get to know her, right?"

"Then why didn't anyone interview Sun Li when he arrived to open the Bamboo Patch? And I don't remember the *Herald* interviewing me when I opened Nevermore Books!"

"Well, I wasn't in town then, but I would have interviewed

you for sure," Vera said, "though I think the fact that Ms. Grey is taking out a big ad might have something to do with it."

"Humph." Lenore ruffled her feathers. She was not the most cheerful of birds. "So what's she like, then? This new mink?"

"She's very classy," Vera said, "but nice as well. She sounds like she's had an interesting life. Born into a family of aristocrats and has all sorts of stories about meeting royalty and such."

Lenore gave a skeptical-sounding squawk. "Oh, indeed? And she gave it all up for Shady Hollow?"

"There's nothing wrong with Shady Hollow," Vera said defensively.

"'Course there is! No place is perfect, and we have bones out in the orchard, don't we? But you're missing my point. There's no reason for a fancy mink to cross the sea and choose our little town for her tea party lessons. So why did she really choose us? Did she say?"

"She just said she liked it," Vera replied with a shrug. "And why not? I liked Shady Hollow when I came here."

"You first came here to research a story, Vera," the raven reminded her, "and you stayed only after you'd been here for a while. You didn't just put your paw on a map and pack your bags. I maintain that this slinky mink must have a reason for coming here. If only I knew a tough investigative reporter who could do a story on that!"

"Oh, please," Vera said. "She's opening an etiquette school, not building an army. And in any case, I'm already working on a story. Those bones have to belong to Julia Elkin. Joe confirmed that this locket"—Vera pulled out the heart-shaped bauble—"is Julia's. It was found right where the bones were unearthed."

Lenore stared at the necklace. She had an eye for shiny objects. "Oh, that's bad news, Vera."

"Why? At least we know for certain."

"But this means there was definitely foul play! Julia was a healthy young moose. She disappeared one night, and now we discover she's been lying dead since then. It's murder, mark my words."

"You're jumping to conclusions. It could have been an accident," Vera said. "I'll go talk to Dr. Broadhead. By now, he might have more to say about the manner of death."

"Ugh. Good luck. What are you doing with that locket? Are you going to give it to Orville?"

"Oh, I suppose I should," Vera said, though she felt reluctant to do so. She thought Orville would also jump to conclusions, which would likely land Joe in a jail cell. "But not quite yet."

"Withholding evidence is serious business, Vera. Not to mention it'll make Orville angry." No one wants to see an angry bear. Ever.

"He won't get mad at me," Vera replied with more confidence than she felt. "And I'll pass it along really soon. Just let me talk to Dr. Broadhead first."

Lenore shrugged. "Okay. It's your funeral."

"Thanks for the support," Vera muttered. "I've got to go."

She sent a message to Dr. Broadhead's office. The snake served as doctor and medical examiner to a huge part of the woodlands and could very well be far from Shady Hollow on any given day. So Vera was a little surprised when a message came back saying that he was available.

She hurried to his office, which, despite being quite warm and half underground—just like her own home—made her flesh crawl. However, he was good at his job, and he'd been around for years.

"Hello, Doctor," Vera began. "I wanted to talk to you about the body found in the orchard."

"Ah, yesss. The moossse. What of it?"

"Well, you did a more thorough examination after that first discovery. I was wondering if you might know how she died."

"Ssshe? How do *you* know it wasss a ssshe?" the snake asked.

"Orville said you told him that the lack of antlers was a clue. Also, I think it was Julia Elkin," Vera said, pulling out the necklace. "This locket was found near the grave around the time of Julia's disappearance."

"Ah. Yesss. Well, it wasss indeed a female moossse. Ssslightly sssmaller than malesss of the sssspecsssiesss. It very well could be Julia who wasss the victim."

"Victim?" Vera asked, steeling herself for the worst.

"Oh, yesss. Mossst csssertainly. The ssskull wasss sssmassshed in with a rock or other hard object. Death mussst have come quickly. But it wasss murder. No quessstion about it."

"Does Orville know this?" she asked.

"Csssertainly. I gave him my full report."

Vera was annoyed that Orville hadn't shared that particular detail with her earlier. It was hardly so inconsequential that it would slip one's mind! Still, that wasn't Dr. Broadhead's fault.

"Well." Vera heaved a sigh. "I guess we should have known. I had hoped—"

"Nothing wrong with hope, but the truth isss the truth no matter what. The victim hasss no more hope, but perhapsss ssshe can have jusssticssse. Will you find it for her, Misss Vixsssen?"

Vera nodded. "I'll try."

Chapter 10

After her talk with the philosophical medical examiner, Vera was more determined than ever to find out what really happened to poor Julia. She was certain that Joe had nothing to do with harming his wife, and she needed to prove it. She decided that a trip to the police station was in order. What else was Orville keeping from her? Did he have a suspect list? More evidence? A theory? All these ideas whirled through Vera's head as she trotted to the station. She was so deep in thought that she almost didn't notice she'd walked into the police station until she was in front of Orville himself, who was standing in the middle of the station, surrounded by neatly arranged bones.

"Watch your step!" he growled.

Vera halted. "Orville," she said in surprise, "what are you doing?" The police bear did not look especially glad to see her.

"I'm tagging each piece of evidence pending further investigation."

"You mean a *murder* investigation! I just came from Dr. Broadhead's office. He told me the skull was smashed in such a way that murder is the only explanation."

"And?" Orville said coolly.

"And I want to know what's going on so I can help find out who killed Julia!"

"You will not, Miss Vixen," he replied.

Oh, dear, this can't be good, Vera thought. He only called her Miss Vixen when he was irritated with her.

Vera began to stammer, but then she gathered her courage and faced the upset bear. She felt like she was back in school, explaining herself to the teacher.

"Deputy Braun," Vera began, willing her voice to remain calm and confident, "I *am* investigating the discovery of Julia Elkin's body—"

Before she could continue, Orville interrupted her. "You are doing nothing of the sort, Miss Vixen," he barked. "This is a police matter, and you work for the newspaper. You are not a detective. I must ask you to stay out of it. And while we're at it, it's probably not such a good idea for us to socialize."

Vera swallowed audibly, not prepared for personal and professional attacks in one go. She couldn't believe he had the nerve to say she wasn't a detective. The events of the summer had already disproved that. Plus, she had the locket—the only real clue so far!

The look on Orville's face told Vera that she had said all

these things aloud. *That's unfortunate,* she thought—silently this time.

"What locket are you talking about?" the bear asked with an edge to his voice. "Vera, I swear, if you're keeping something from me, I . . ." He sputtered and went silent.

"I didn't go looking for it," she responded, realizing just how angry Orville was. "Winifred, one of the rabbits at the orchard, gave it to me. *She* came to *me.* I was going to show it to you, but I hadn't got around to it yet."

Vera pulled the old locket out of her bag and handed it to Orville. She wanted to throw it in his face, but she refrained. In fact, she thought she had shown admirable restraint through-out their entire interaction.

Orville took the locket and opened the silver heart. He sighed when he saw the picture of the younger Joe on the inside. "Did Joe confirm this is his wife's locket?"

"Yes," Vera said, "and based on the fact that it was found in the same location during the same summer when the body was buried, there's no more question, is there?"

"The body must be Julia Elkin's. Broadhead's laboratory tests say death was between ten and twelve years ago. The decay of the bones tells us that," Orville said.

"So what's the next step?" Vera asked. Knowing the victim was a resident of the Hollow was different from guessing it. The town would be shocked to hear it and would want the murder solved as soon as possible.

"The next step, Miss Vixen?" Vera could tell that Orville was struggling to keep his temper in check. "I want you to sign a statement saying where you got that locket and then leave the statement and the locket with me," he said, "and then I want you to keep out of this investigation. I am handling it, and I will find out who killed Julia Elkin. Am I clear?"

Vera nodded meekly, but inside she was livid. He couldn't tell her what to do. She could investigate whatever she chose. What's more, she would solve this case before Orville and free Joe of any suspicion. As for her relationship with the infuriating police bear—it was done. She did not need a controlling partner who doubted her abilities. She could not believe how angry she was.

Vera wrote out a statement and signed it with a flourish. "There you go. Good day, Deputy," she said as she turned to go. She would not cry until she was well away from Orville and out of view of any other creature who might observe her.

But by the time Vera had left the station, she had changed her mind about crying. She was still incensed, and her anger increased the farther she walked. How dare he suggest that she was not a detective! That was half her job as a journalist. She was constantly investigating facts and checking out stories. As for no more socializing, that was just *fine*. She had no interest in being seen with that bungling excuse for a police bear! If it weren't for Joe, she would stay out of this case completely and let Orville fumble his way through it. But Joe was her friend, and she had no intention of letting him be convicted of a murder that he did not commit.

All of a sudden, Vera stopped walking and looked around. She had been so consumed that she had gone completely out of her way. She realized that she had just passed the home of Howard Chitters and his enormous family. Behind the main house was a small structure where Howard's elderly grandfather resided—and indeed had resided for decades. He was a very old field mouse but still maintained his independence and made all his own meals. Vera wondered what he might remember about Julia Elkin and her disappearance.

Deciding there's no time like the present, Vera approached the apartment behind the house and knocked gently on the door. She did not want to disturb the old gentlemouse if he was taking a nap.

To her surprise, the door opened almost immediately, and a gray field mouse stood there. "Yes?" he said. "May I help you?"

Vera introduced herself and then said, "Do you mind if I ask you a few questions?"

"Of course not," replied the mouse. "This is the most interesting thing to happen to me in weeks."

He led her to the porch, which held a few chairs and a table with an umbrella. Determining that one of the tiny mouse-sized chairs would not hold a fox, albeit a petite one, Vera decided to stand.

"Thank you so much for your time, Mr. Chitters—" she began.

"Call me Luther," the mouse interrupted. "It's not every day that a pretty young creature stops by my house."

Vera let that one go, although after her spat with Orville, it was nice to be appreciated. She whipped out her notebook and looked thoughtfully at the elderly mouse.

"I'm looking into the disappearance of Julia Elkin," she began. "Do you remember when she came to town with her husband, Joe?"

"Of course," replied Luther. "Moose—such enormous creatures! We had never had any in Shady Hollow before. Some townsfolk were frightened of them at first." Seeing the questioning look in Vera's eyes, the mouse continued, "Oh, it didn't last long. Once we got to know them, we learned how kind and gentle they were. At least, how Joe was."

"What about Julia?" asked Vera. "Wasn't she nice?"

"Well," Luther replied slowly, as if gathering his thoughts, "not really. She was always polite, but you got the feeling that she was just doing it for show. Not like she really cared. Not like Joe."

Vera knew what he meant. Joe knew the names of all his customers and their favorite items to order and the names of most of their relatives. On your first visit to Joe's Mug, you felt as if he truly was happy to see you and to serve you a drink. It was the kind of thing that could not be faked. Although it seemed Julia had tried.

"Does that mean you didn't talk with her much?" Vera asked. She'd been hoping that someone was aware of Julia's movements during the last days of her life.

"Only the sort of hello, goodbye I give everyone," Luther admitted. "Julia didn't find much in common with me, you understand. I'm a mouse, and I've never set a paw beyond this woodland in my whole life! Not exactly a kindred spirit. She wasn't happy in one spot."

"Did she mention that?"

"Didn't have to. Moose voices can grow to quite a bellow, you know. I heard her and Joe arguing some nights. She wanted to move on. He didn't. What would Joe's Mug be without Joe? He had to stay!"

Vera twitched her nose—a sure sign that she was thinking hard. The account of a bickering couple didn't exactly cast a good light on Joe in the wake of Julia's death. But then again, Luther's version confirmed what Joe had told her. Wasn't it reassuring that Joe hadn't lied about their relationship?

"Poor Joe," Luther continued. "The café took all his attention, and he didn't even have a chance to patch things up before it was too late."

"What do you mean?" Vera asked.

"Julia had packed a bag a few weeks before she disappeared. I saw her carry it past the house late one evening. I'm not a sound sleeper . . . didn't sleep much even back then, and that summer was terribly hot. Even the nights were oppressive. That's why I was awake and on the porch at the late hour. I saw her haul it along—a big old suitcase with red flowers all over it. About a half hour later, she came back along the path but without the bag. She must have hidden it in the woods to be ready for when she left."

"I wonder where she intended to go," Vera said.

"Somewhere pretty far away, to judge by the size of the bag. When she did stop to say hello those last few weeks, I recall she was rather pleasant. Maybe the idea of running away made her a little more polite in the end. Like she knew it was all going to be over, so chatting with a neighbor wasn't going to kill her. Um, so to speak."

"Did she chat with anyone else?"

"Not that I saw, but then I don't leave my bailiwick much." He patted the porch rail affectionately. "She mentioned a friend who she was planning something grand with . . . a good friend, I suppose. But I never caught a name."

"Thanks, Luther. You've been a big help."

Vera went home, full of thoughts about all she'd learned that day. Everything seemed to circle around Julia's unhappiness. But still, there was no connection between Julia and Cold Clay Orchards. If she had run away, why did her body end up in the orchard? Who found her there that hot summer night? Vera had no answers and finally fell into an exhausted doze.

The next morning, Vera was awoken by a tapping, as of someone gently rapping on her chamber door. Grumbling, she got up and padded over. "Hold on, hold on, I'm coming."

Lenore stood outside, ready to put her beak to the door again. She blinked upon seeing Vera and promptly dropped a newspaper at the fox's feet.

"You're going to want to know about this," she said in a bleak tone, which, for Lenore, was saying something.

"What happened?" Vera asked, scooping up the paper. Had another body been discovered?

She scanned the headline, reading only "New Business Promises Polite Future." It was her interview with Octavia. A quick read suggested that nothing much had been changed from the text she'd given BW. "This is all right, I think. BW didn't mess it up."

"Not that," Lenore said impatiently. "Gossip column."

"You know I don't ever read that." Vera prided herself on remaining above such idle topics.

"You'll want to today."

Vera flipped a few pages until she reached Gladys Honeysuckle's column and then surveyed the tidbits. " 'Canoe Canoodling: Couples Caught at Mirror Lake.' 'Raccoon Riches: Lolly Haversham Inherits Everything, Cousins Cut Out of Will.' 'Pass the Plate: Edith von Beaverpelt Announces Charity Tea Party.' 'Romance Arrested: *Vixen and Braun on the Outs*'?!" Vera spat the last words, her paws shaking as she reread the line.

How did Gladys even know what happened? "That busybody hummingbird! How dare she? I'm going to set her tailfeathers on fire! I'll toss her into the presses! I'll drown her in the ink vats!"

"Steady on, Vera." The raven spread her wings to force Vera back inside her den. "I just wanted you to know what you're in for today. I'm not suggesting you go and attack anyone."

"Oh, this is so embarrassing!" Vera threw the paper on the floor. "What sort of sneaky, conniving creature would write that about a colleague? It's intolerable!" She suddenly remembered how annoyed Gladys had been that Vera knew about the bones before she did. This was retaliation, pure and simple.

"Do you want a cup of tea?" Lenore asked, still using her wings to block Vera from leaving the safety of her home.

"Tea? I don't want tea, I want justice!"

"Well, I can do a cup of tea," Lenore said.

Vera stalked over to her favorite chair and collapsed into it. "Yes. Tea. Might as well. I can't go into the office today, not after this."

Lenore added water to the kettle and put it on the stove. "Don't be a goose. You've got to go in no matter what. Facing it down is the only way. If you hide, folks will assume you've got something to conceal. What happened, by the way? This bit of news can't have come from nowhere."

"Orville and I had a fight yesterday. He found out about the locket, and he was so angry at me for not giving it over sooner. He virtually accused me of hiding evidence. And he forbade me from continuing my investigation!"

"That was the anger talking," the raven said. "He knows you well enough to know that you're not going to do *that*."

"The station doors were open. Gladys must have overheard

us talking. Or someone else did and then told her. This is mortifying, Lenore! What am I supposed to say to Orville?"

"About the gossip column? Nothing. It's not your fault any more than it's his. Folks should fight behind closed doors if they don't want others to know their business."

"Joe and Julia fought behind closed doors. Seems folks knew about it anyway."

"Did you learn something?" Lenore asked.

Over a bracing cup of tea, Vera related all that the mouse Luther Chitters had told her. "Seems Julia was definitely intending to leave town on her own—so that's not the question. The question is who crossed her path while she was on the way out?"

"Joe had motive," Lenore admitted somberly. "He could have found out she was leaving, chased after her, and killed her in a rage. Think about it. He buries the body in some far corner of the orchard, then tells folks that Julia just up and left. Who's to think otherwise? If he did it, he probably never dreamed the body would be dug up, not after all this time."

"If he knew his wife's body lay in the orchard, would he keep making pies out of Cold Clay fruit? That would be dark."

Lenore, an acknowledged expert on all things dark, nodded somberly. "That it would be. Though, for what it's worth, I still don't believe Joe is a cold-blooded killer. Perhaps it was an accident."

"Oh, please. Are you suggesting Julia fell over and then thoughtfully buried herself?" Vera growled. "Anyway, Dr. Broadhead told me that the damage to the skull meant someone had struck her with a rock or something heavy. Nope. This is murder, all right."

"Then that means there's a murderer in Shady Hollow.

Again." Lenore sighed. "We'll have to catch them. But first you've got to go to the *Herald*'s offices and show your face. Then you can leave to do the investigation. Come on, it's time. I have to open the bookshop!"

The two friends made their way to the center of town. Lenore said goodbye to Vera on the doorstep of Nevermore Books, promising she'd be there if and when Vera needed a spot to retreat to after her showdown with Gladys.

"Don't do anything you'll regret," Lenore warned.

"We'll see." Vera wasn't about to go easy on the gossipy hummingbird.

Vera walked into the newspaper office. Even at this early hour, the place was loud and bustling—such was the nature of the business. But throughout the newsroom, ears pricked up and glances were exchanged as creatures prepared themselves for a battle. One rabbit bearing a trayful of letterpress blocks realized she was exactly between Vera's and Gladys's desks. She froze in place, staring at the furious fox with wide, terrified eyes. Another rabbit reached out and pulled her out of danger before the type blocks could spill onto the floor.

Gladys saw Vera, of course. She fluttered her wings faster than ever, perhaps to hide the state of nervousness she was in. "Oh, hello, Vera," she peeped. "Er, um. Nice morning, isn't it?"

Vera took a deep breath, looked Gladys in the eye . . . and then simply walked on by. She ignored the bird completely, not even offering an insult. Instead, Vera walked slowly to her own desk, put her things down, and sat in her chair. She very deliberately took pen and paper and began to write out some notes. In truth, she was merely scribbling—she barely had words to describe her anger, but she remembered Lenore's advice not to do anything she'd regret. And anything she might say to Gladys just then would be *very* regrettable.

Over the next few moments, while Vera continued to write meaningless phrases, the sense of tension throughout the newsroom slowly faded and the normal bustle resumed.

"My dear," a smooth voice murmured next to her ear, "that was one of the finest examples of the cut direct that I have ever been privileged to witness."

Vera spun her chair around to see Octavia standing there. The mink was watching her with an almost-reverential expression.

"What's a cut direct?" Vera asked.

"Come with me and I'll tell you." Octavia pivoted, and as she did so, her sleek silvery coat caught the light along with the gazes of several workers. Vera got up and followed her toward BW Stone's office.

"The cut direct," Octavia explained in a quiet tone as they walked, "is a supremely useful social tool. It is the simple act of not acknowledging your opponent while still making clear that you know she is present. To look into your opponent's eyes and then disdain to engage . . . a powerful, and even devastating, move. In fact, it is difficult to play well. Most folks overexaggerate how they ignore the other or cannot resist a quick comment. But you, my dear . . . you did it perfectly!"

Vera smiled a little despite the situation. "Thank you."

"Ah, I should thank you for the opportunity to see it. And of course your victim is a gossip columnist. That only makes it more rewarding. Paparazzi and the like are contemptible." Octavia sniffed, as though merely acknowledging that gossip existed was a bit distasteful.

At the moment, Vera was inclined to agree. It would be a long while before she gave Gladys the time of day!

They reached BW's office; the skunk was waiting. "Come in and we'll discuss the latest idea of yours, Ms. Grey. How exciting! Vera, you don't know what you're in for!"

Vera blanched. What had BW gotten her into now?

Chapter 11

Vera could only imagine what kind of idea Octavia and her boss had cooked up, but at least it would distract her from the gossip column. This was one of the drawbacks of living in a small town like Shady Hollow—folks know your business. In a city, absolutely no creature would care if two random citizens ended their romance, even if they conducted their personal lives in a public forum. City dwellers are too wrapped up in themselves to care about what's going on with their neighbors. Vera enjoyed being part of the community in the village where she currently resided, but today she wished for anonymity. It was difficult enough to think about things ending with Orville, but it was decidedly worse to be a subject of town gossip and speculation. She really would like to strangle that hummingbird!

Vera came out of her thoughts to find BW and Octavia both looking at her expectantly. *Oh, no,* she thought. *Have they been talking this whole time? I didn't hear a thing.*

There was no way to get out of this one. The fox could not react to a plan that she had not heard. She shook herself and apologized. "I'm terribly sorry," she began, "but I got very little sleep last night, and I have a bit of a headache. Could you please go over the situation again for me?"

The skunk and the mink exchanged a look, but that was all. Stone removed the cold cigar he had been chomping on from between his teeth and sighed audibly. Vera was supposed to be his star reporter.

"Ms. Grey has a fantastic idea," he said, apparently for the second time. "You will attend classes at the new etiquette school and write a series of stories about your experience."

"There will, of course, be no charge to you," continued Octavia, as if this were a huge incentive. "You may attend a sampling of courses—table manners, elocution, ballroom dancing—the possibilities are endless!"

Vera would rather be drawn and quartered than take ballroom dancing lessons, but she tried to appear excited. She knew from experience that once BW Stone had his heart set on something, there would be no getting out of it. Her stern employer appeared to be completely smitten by this newcomer.

Vera realized that the sooner she agreed to this insipid plan, the sooner she could get out of Stone's office and the sooner she could continue looking for Julia's murderer.

"Sounds like a terrific idea," she offered, summoning as

much enthusiasm as she could. "I look forward to working with you, Ms. Grey."

"Oh, you must call me Octavia," the mink purred in response. Either she was completely over the moon about working with Vera or she was an award-winning actress. Vera did not care which was true at this point. She just wanted to concentrate on her case.

"Sure thing. Listen, Octavia, I'll be in touch about the details. You'll have to excuse me. I'm on a deadline for another story," Vera said, and then made her exit as gracefully as possible. She did not wait to see if either one of the creatures believed her.

Once she was safely in the hallway outside Stone's office, Vera took a deep breath and got herself together. Then, instead of returning to her desk, she slipped out the back door of the *Herald*'s offices and made her way swiftly to Nevermore Books.

One might expect that Vera would calm down on the walk to the bookstore to see her friend. However, she only got more and more worked up. She reached the shop and pushed open the door with a bang, raising quite a bit of dust and startling Lenore, who was working on the accounts in her tiny office. Sunlight streamed in from the high windows, creating a beautiful effect that was utterly lost on the fox.

"Goodness, Vera!" sputtered the raven once she reached the ground floor. "What has happened now?"

"You will not believe this!" hollered Vera, unable to control her anger.

"Vera, Vera," soothed Lenore, "please try to calm down while I make you a cup of tea. Nothing could be that bad."

The fox realized that she was yelling at her friend in her place of business, and she tried to relax. She climbed the stairs to the third level and, her tail swishing, paced back and forth in the social criticism section (she felt it appropriate) while Lenore fetched the tea.

When her friend returned with the tea tray, Vera had calmed down enough to explain how she was to be an etiquette student in order to write a series of articles. The raven did not react in quite the way that Vera expected.

"Sounds interesting enough." The raven shrugged. "You'll do fine—you always do. Although I do think your time might be better spent looking for the suitcase Julia had just before she disappeared."

"Lenore! Are you serious?" Vera said. "Can you see me ballroom dancing? I'm a detective!"

"No," Lenore countered sharply, to the surprise of the fox. "You're a reporter, and *this* is your job. After all, it could be much worse. Remember your piece on the stomach-flu outbreak at the middle school last year?"

"Don't remind me," Vera replied with a shudder.

"Etiquette classes might even be fun. And they will take your mind off any troubles you're having with a certain police bear. You might even meet someone new."

"In Shady Hollow?" Vera snorted at this, but she was beginning to see things in perspective. She would take classes at the etiquette school to make Stone happy, and she would still investigate the moose's murder. After all, she wouldn't be spending her evenings canoodling with Orville, and that left plenty of time for her investigation. Leave it to Lenore to take a different view on things. Vera was so glad that she and the raven were friends. It meant everything to her. No matter what happened in her career or her romantic life, she knew that she could count on the raven to be there for her, and vice versa.

Vera rubbed her paws over her ears to straighten her ruffled fur. "Well, since I don't have to attend a class on introducing a baronet to a marchioness yet, let's look for that suitcase tonight. Meet me on the northern edge of the millpond path—that's close to Joe's home—and we'll retrace Julia's possible route."

"I'll be there!" Lenore said. "And first I'll do some research in the mystery section on how to best conduct a search."

For a bird, Lenore sure was a grounded creature. With that promise, Vera left the bookshop feeling much more herself.

The calm feeling lasted until she caught a glimpse of Orville walking in the opposite direction down Main Street. Having no desire to talk to him, Vera ducked into a little alley between two buildings where she could hide until there was no chance of Orville's turning around and seeing her. From what little she'd seen, he was in a dour mood. Creatures coming the other way took notice and politely veered out of his path to avoid a confrontation. Orville was, by and large, well liked and respected in the town, but that didn't mean folks wanted to face him when he was out of sorts.

Vera knew Orville must have read that morning's paper as well; he made a point to know all the happenings around town. He had to be as annoyed by the gossip column as she was. Perhaps one day they could commiserate about it . . . but not today.

Since Vera didn't want to hang about town and face the scrutiny of others, she chose to head out into the woods for a calming walk. Who knew? Maybe she'd find another clue. One of the last buildings on Maple Street—beyond that point the town petered out, forming outskirts and then merging into the woods—was the Bamboo Patch. Vera's pace slowed as she passed, thinking she ought to say hello to the restaurant's proprietor, the panda Sun Li. He was an even more recent transplant to Shady Hollow than Vera, and she wondered what he might think of all this news of death. His perspective was frequently useful.

A flash of white emerged from behind the green stalks of bamboo growing in front of the restaurant. The panda had just stepped outside, and he lifted a paw in greeting.

"Hello, Sun Li!" Vera called. "How are you?"

"Hard at work," the panda replied. "Actually, do you have a moment? I could use a little assistance."

Vera turned down the little pebbled path to the Bamboo Patch's front door. "Of course. What do you need?"

"Come inside and I'll show you."

Vera expected that Sun Li needed help with moving something or some other similar chore, even though the bear was far stronger than she. However, he led her to a table in the dining area and sat her in front of a covered dish. With a little flourish, he lifted the lid, and a puff of fragrant steam wafted upward.

"Try this," said Sun Li.

Vera tasted the dish eagerly. It was nothing more than steamed rice, but it was spiced with cinnamon and cloves and had little cubes of winter squash mixed in.

"Sun Li," she said, "this is fantastic!"

"Yes," he said modestly, "I thought so. I've been experimenting with spices since I got an incorrect shipment last month. These aren't usual flavors for me, but I'm branching out. I wanted a second opinion on the dish."

"I second the opinion that you should list it on the menu." Vera licked the plate, inhaling the last of the savory cinnamon. "And keep on branching! How's business, by the way?"

"Going well," Sun Li said. "The cooler months mean more customers. Folk are thinking about the harvest and getting padded for winter." He rubbed his own belly, perhaps thinking of all the good food to come.

"I'm worried that Joe is about to hit a rough patch," Vera said. "This news about the bones belonging to Julia could be bad for him." She related the latest public information about the case; she knew Sun Li wasn't as quick to hear about news as some others in town.

Sun Li pondered for a moment but then said, "I wouldn't worry too much. Joe's established himself, and folks know him well. I bet he'll actually see an increase in customers coming to support him."

"But what if . . . there's something that looks incriminating?"

"Vera, your nose is twitching, and that means you're already on the case. I'm sure you'll get to the bottom of it and Joe won't have a thing to worry about."

"Hope you're right." Vera stood up. "Well, I'll let you get back to work."

"Take a walk," he advised. "Sometimes all you need to see clearly is something new to look at."

Vera smiled, pleased that Sun Li's recommendation was what she'd told herself earlier, even if he put it better.

Vera left the Bamboo Patch, trailing her paws along the hollow bamboo stems lining the pathway and tapping the big tubes as if they were instruments. Then she wandered into the forest among the familiar oaks and elms. More were turning yellow and orange by the day. She sniffed at a faint smell of smoke in the air; even though she couldn't see the town, she knew it was close.

Once again, it struck her as odd that Julia had been discovered in the orchard. If Julia had been leaving, why go all the way *through* town—as she evidently must have done—in order to get *away* from town? It made no sense.

"She must have had an errand," Vera said out loud. "Something she had to do before she left for good. But what?"

All through her walk, Vera racked her brain but couldn't think of a reason for the orchard to be on Julia's list. And yet she'd clearly been there.

"Maybe the suitcase will tell us," Vera said to herself. With that in mind, she hurried to meet Lenore, who was waiting near Joe's house.

"At the appointed hour, right on time!" the raven said, ruffling her glossy black feathers. "Let's retrace Julia's likely route into the woods."

Vera nodded. "If we can find any hint of her plans in that suitcase, we might find a clue to the murderer."

"It's a long shot. If the case is still here, it's been years. Wind, rain, cold . . ."

"I know," Vera said, "but we have to try."

"Agreed."

"Let's put ourselves in Julia's hooves," Vera began. "Then we can figure out which route is the most likely one for her to have taken."

"All right," Lenore said. "Here goes: I'm a moose. I'm an unhappy wife and mother, I don't like my job, and I can't wait to get out of town." She paused. "Sorry. I'm trying to get into a moose's frame of mind, and it's difficult. When I want to go somewhere, I just fly!"

"True enough," Vera said. "Let's try to imagine her actions, though. Luther Chitters said it was late when Julia walked by with her suitcase. She was trying to avoid being seen by anyone. Most likely, she slipped out of the house, made her way to the woods here, and then put the suitcase in a place where she could easily get it when she was ready to leave Shady Hollow. Luther was a fluke, but maybe someone else saw her that night, too, like Professor Heidegger." Vera made a mental note to interview the scholarly owl later that evening.

"The least-populated path to the woods is that way," Lenore said, pointing with her wing.

Vera and Lenore went carefully from Joe's house toward the woods. Vera walked and Lenore flew at a very low altitude. Autumn was advancing, and piles of bright-colored leaves and dry brush lay everywhere. Vera checked a few of the larger piles, wondering if an item such as a suitcase could remain hidden in such a place for so many years. Then again, it was also possible that another creature could have found it at some point later on and taken it; in that case, the suitcase was gone forever.

"This might be a wild-goose chase," Vera called to the airborne Lenore.

"Probably. But we'll try until the light fails," the raven cawed back. "It's the proper thing to do."

The fox and the raven ventured deeper and deeper into the forest. It was very quiet and just beginning to get dark. Vera was not afraid, but she was ever so slightly on edge. Whenever a murder occurred, one was reminded that one did not ever really know one's neighbors.

They searched tree hollows and rock stacks and spinneys. Vera was almost ready to give up and call it a night when Lenore, who had flown higher for a better look at their surroundings, pointed out a prospective pile of thick brush at the base of an extremely large and old oak tree. Vera was tired and dirty, but she supposed that it would not hurt to examine one last pile. She began rifling through the sticks and leaves with her front paws, pulling at the larger branches. Lenore hovered anxiously above her to provide encouragement and moral support.

Suddenly Vera's left paw struck something hard. Not wanting to get her hopes up, she said nothing to her friend but continued to dig, trying to unearth whatever she had struck. Then she began to get excited as, little by little, a rectangular object emerged from under the decaying leaves at the bottom of the pile. It *had* to be Julia's suitcase. It couldn't be anything else!

Though the mysterious buried object was too heavy for Vera to move, she continued to uncover it, removing debris from all around.

Lenore fluttered down. "Well? Is it Julia's?"

Vera brushed off the outside. "A big case with red flowers, just like Luther said. It is!"

Lenore and Vera exchanged a look. The excitement in the air was palpable. They had discovered Julia's missing suitcase! Here was the proof that Julia had definitely planned to leave her family and the town of Shady Hollow. But why hadn't she retrieved the case the night she'd left home? What had happened to derail her plans?

Fortunately the suitcase was not locked, and Vera had no trouble unlatching its rusty hooks. As the lid swung upward, Vera felt her insides clench with anticipation.

At first all the amateur detectives could see was some rumpled clothing, now moldy and moth-eaten. This was mildly disappointing, but, after all, it is what one should expect to find in a suitcase. Vera pushed the clothing aside and burrowed into the corners of the case. There was a small framed picture of an extremely young moose that could only be Joe Junior, a book entitled *The Road to Charmville*, and some outdated travel guides for distant lands.

"Where's Charmville?" Vera asked, looking at the book's warped cover. It was covered in green buckram, now mildewed.

"Somewhere sunnier, no doubt," the raven said. "I've never heard of the place."

Vera kept digging and finally revealed a stack of handwritten letters bundled together with string.

"Lenore!" she said excitedly. "Letters!" Vera deduced that any clue they might find would lie in the contents of the letters—if they were still legible.

"Let's get somewhere warm and light to read them. Not the bookstore, though, because we might have to hide them in a hurry."

"We'll go to my house," Vera said. They'd read the letters first, and then Vera would let Orville know about the find. She wouldn't let him accuse her of obstruction again. The suitcase had been hidden for so many years that a few more hours would make no difference. Vera snatched up the packet of letters, the picture, and the book and carefully closed and covered the suitcase again. Tomorrow she'd tell Orville where it was so the authorities could come collect it. Then she and Lenore made their way back to her house to see what they'd discovered.

When the fox and the raven got back to Vera's cottage, they wasted no time checking out the contents of Julia's correspondence. Vera thought about making tea but changed her mind and poured two small glasses of port instead. She carried the drinks out to her small living room, where Lenore was waiting with the packet of letters. She gave one glass to Lenore, who took a grateful sip.

"Good hunting." Vera toasted her friend. "To think that suitcase was there for ten years!"

"Eleven," Lenore corrected.

Vera sat down in the wing chair opposite Lenore's on the other side of the tiny fireplace and took a fortifying taste of the port. Then she picked up the first letter from the top of the stack. An overwhelming odor of must and mildew made her sneeze.

"Ugh! These smell like a swamp."

"They'll dry out," Lenore said, examining a letter of her own.

Vera studied the paper in her paws closely. As expected, it was addressed to Julia. Her name and address were written in a spiky formal hand. There was no return address, and the postmark was blurred and faded. Vera opened the envelope eagerly and pulled out two densely written pages. She looked at the bottom of the second page to check the signature. Disappointingly, the letter was signed only *Your dear friend*. How aggravating! The letter could be from anyone!

"The earliest date I see is May," Vera noted, riffling through the letters, "but it sounds like the writers knew each other pretty well by that point."

"Yes," Lenore agreed. "We've got only one slice of the correspondence, not to mention only one side of it. I wish we knew what Julia was saying all this time." She waved a damp letter in the air to help it dry.

The friends soldiered on. Vera would have to read through

each letter carefully to see if they contained any clues pointing to Julia's murderer. Lenore was trying to look alert, but Vera knew the bird was tired. Lenore had been up early to work on the accounts at her store, then she'd stocked the shelves and dusted before spending most of the day dealing with customers.

"You should go home, Lenore," Vera advised her friend. "This might take all night. I'll do it. Why not get some rest? I'll tell you if I find something."

Lenore looked relieved, said good night, and slipped out the front door. Vera didn't worry about the raven getting home safely, as she knew Lenore's home was only a brief flight away.

Once Lenore was gone, Vera turned back to the letters. She wasn't that tired, and she wanted to find a clue. This correspondence must've been very important, or Julia wouldn't have bothered to pack it in her one suitcase. Vera had realized immediately that Julia wasn't running away with a lover. These could not be love letters. No one would sign a love letter *Your dear friend*. (Vera did not have much experience with love letters, but she was confident this was true.)

She started to read, learning of a creature who was as lonely and restless as Julia.

A few hours later, Vera woke up with a letter stuck to her face. Apparently she was not the tireless detective she'd thought. Bother! She would go to bed and read the letters properly when she was more awake.

The next day, Vera slept in and was a bit late getting to the office. She hurried to her desk, deposited her bag, and walked over to the counter where a pot of hot (indeed rather scorched) coffee always sat. She was pouring herself a mug when the rabbit Barry Greenfield walked up to her. "Big news, huh, Vera?"

"Oh, what now?"

Barry's ears fluttered as if of their own accord. "You haven't heard? Joe's been arrested."

"Arrested?" Vera gasped. "Do you mean Orville took him in for more questioning?"

"No, sweetheart, I mean Joe's been arrested. Charged with murder. Bit odd that your—ahem—close contacts at the police station didn't tip you off before the fact."

"Oh, hush up." Vera was so shocked at the news, she let Barry's *sweetheart* slide right by. Not that Barry would change his habits at this point in his life. "What could Orville be thinking?"

"Maybe you can find a reporter somewhere around here to chase that lead." Barry touched a paw to his nose and strolled off.

Well. Vera didn't need any more encouragement than that. She hurried as fast as she could to the police station without drawing attention to herself. The last thing she wanted to do was to run into anyone who wanted to speculate about whether Joe was a murderer. Vera knew in her heart that he was not, but knowing it and proving it were two very different things.

Why did Orville choose to actually *arrest* Joe? He couldn't possibly have any substantial evidence. The faster Vera walked, the angrier she became. How could Orville imagine for a minute that gentle Joe had murdered anyone? She knew Orville did his job as he saw fit, but she longed to inform him—in a most unprofessional manner—that he was making a huge mistake and that he should concentrate on finding the real killer.

There was a small crowd in front of the police station—mostly folks muttering to one another about the news and whether this meant no more specialty pies on Thursdays.

That's your main concern? Vera wanted to ask. Instead she put her head down and plowed through the crush, yelling, "Move aside! Press coming through! Thank you!"

"Vera, what's the story?" a chipmunk called in a squeaky voice.

"Working on it, Ben!" Vera responded without looking back. She pushed open the doors of the station and slid through, closing them behind her.

"No comment!" a voice boomed out.

That comment came from Chief Meade, who was making a rare appearance in the station. The chief adjusted his cap and looked down at Vera from his vantage point. "Miss Vixen, you'd best be off. We're very busy here."

Vera looked over to the cells. Joe, looking resigned, occupied the nearest one. The space was hardly large enough for him to stand upright, let alone be comfortable. "Hello, Joe," she said, disregarding the chief. "Interesting day?"

Joe nodded. "Could say that." His rack pinged against the iron bars. "Could say a few other things, too. But I won't."

"The suspect hasn't said anything," Orville growled from where he was standing by the cells.

"That's his right," Vera reminded the bear. She looked at Joe again. "Shall I call a lawyer for you, Joe?"

"Mr. Fallow is on his way, but thank you."

Hearing that news relieved Vera. The rat Mr. Fallow knew his business. She pulled out her notebook, turning back to Chief Meade. "I'll be writing an article on this. I'll need a copy of the arrest report, of course, and any comments the police care to make."

"No comment!" Meade repeated. He sounded quite agitated as he spoke, and he kept peeking at the crowd outside. "Orville, disperse these folks. They're blocking the entrance. Why are they here, anyway? They should be happy we've made an arrest!"

Orville gestured for Vera to come to his desk. He handed her a copy of the arrest report and said, "The orders from Chief Meade are clear. In light of the evidence of a troubled marriage and Julia's disappearance eleven years ago and the recovery of her body this week, we've arrested Joe Elkin on the charge of murder."

"Oh, Orville," Vera said, unable to hide her disappointment.

Orville bent his head, saying, in a much lower voice, "You can't print this next bit, Vera. Meade insisted I arrest *some*body, and Joe is the only suspect. Meade wants it understood that the police are on top of the matter."

"But you don't think Joe did it!" Vera guessed.

"If he's innocent, he'll be fine." Orville's expression was one of extreme doubt.

Meade said, more loudly, "Deputy! Clear that crowd!"

"Yes, sir." Orville pointed Vera toward the back of the police station. "You might want to take the back door. It'll be chaotic in the front."

Vera nodded. After a final encouraging wave to Joe, she left the police station through the back door and emerged into a narrow alleyway. She heard bellowing from the street—

Orville's crowd control. She chose to go in the opposite direction, to where the alley opened onto Apple Street.

Vera would have to work fast if she was going to find the real killer. She did not believe for a second that Joe was capable of murdering his wife, burying her body, and then lying about it for over a decade. It was inconceivable. But an arrest meant the police were serious about someone answering for the crime.

She was sure they had the wrong someone.

Chapter 12

The next morning arrived so dreary and gray that Vera simply wanted to curl her tail around herself and go back to sleep. But sleep wasn't going to help Joe. She rolled out of bed, rustled up a simple breakfast of dried fruit and cheese, and then picked up the stack of letters once more, ready to search for clues.

She had her trusty notebook beside her, and she wrote down a number of questions as she studied the letters. Who was *Your dear friend*? How had the friend and Julia met? What was Julia's plan, and did this mysterious friend play a part in it?

The answer to the last question seemed to be yes. The letters Vera possessed were written over a span of three months or so, and all pointed to the friend and Julia traveling somewhere far away: a big city near the coast. They were going to start up a new business—fashion—that would make them both wealthy. The mysterious friend was a persuasive writer. Even Vera got a little excited by the idea of fabulous clothing, famous clients, and yards and yards of fine silks and satins. It sounded incredibly glamorous.

However, fashion didn't sound like something Julia Elkin knew very much about. No one had spoken about Julia being a moose of style. Perhaps the friend would bring the style. But if that were the case, what was Julia to bring?

The second-to-last letter suggested an answer:

> *How clever you are, Julia! If you retrieve the funds*
> *in the manner you suggest, then we will have plenty*
> *to begin our venture, and no one will miss it until*
> *well after you are gone. Take heart—your ordeal*
> *will not last much longer.*

The fox wrinkled her nose thoughtfully. So Julia had been trying to get hold of some money before her departure, and it sounded as if she didn't plan to wander into Main Street Bank and clear out her account.

"She was going to steal the money," Vera guessed out loud. Theft was a serious matter, though it sounded like Julia had grown desperate. But what did she want to steal? From where? From whom? If she carried out the theft, it would have been discovered, even if no one connected it to Julia.

Vera looked at the date of the letter again. That was her

clue. She could go to the *Herald*'s archives and look through the papers from that month and year. Any theft ought to have been covered in an article.

Her path now set, Vera bounded out of her den with new energy. She forgot Gladys's infuriating column from the other day, forgot that she wasn't on speaking terms with Orville, and even forgot to grab a hot drink at Joe's before entering the newspaper office.

She greeted the few folk she met with a brief buzzy "Good morning!" and then dashed along before anyone could actually ask questions. She bypassed her desk and immediately descended the stairs to the building's underground levels and the archives, which held various useful books and every edition of the newspaper, all lovingly stored for posterity and research.

The space was quite dark and occupied mostly with shelves in long narrow rows. In the closest corner were a few desks and tables. An elderly rabbit sat at one; a metal nameplate on the front of the desk announced her as MRS. BINSLEY. She peered at Vera with sharp, inquisitive eyes.

"How may I help you?"

"Hello," said Vera. "I need the papers from the month of July eleven years ago. The whole month. It's important."

"Vera Vixen, is it? The new reporter?"

Vera had been reporting in Shady Hollow for well over a year, but she nodded. "Yes, ma'am. I'm researching a story. I need to know more about the time when Julia Elkin disappeared."

"She left here in August, not July."

There was nothing wrong with the rabbit's memory, that was for sure.

"True, but I think something might have happened in town in July that will help us understand Julia's actions."

"I'll bring out July's papers, day by day." The archivist vanished into the dim stacks.

Vera expected it would take a long time for the rabbit to return, but it was only a few minutes before she came back. She was carefully wheeling a cart stacked with a few old issues of the *Herald*.

"You can look at these at a table. One at a time. When you need more, I'll fetch them."

"Thanks. I don't suppose you've got any coffee around here? It would warm me up."

The aged rabbit tapped one hind foot on the cold floor. "Absolutely no food or drink in the archives. That's rule number two."

"Oh." Vera sighed. Then she asked, "What's rule number one?"

"Rule number one is whatever I say it is."

"Yes, ma'am," Vera said meekly. If she'd learned only one lesson as a cub reporter, it was this: Never cross a librarian. You might not come out of the stacks again.

So, sans coffee, she paged carefully through the old papers that the rabbit brought out every so often. Vera wrote down every reference to a theft, no matter how petty, as well as any reference to Joe or Julia. Nothing seemed too remarkable, however. Then, in an edition dated late July, she found something interesting.

"The von Beaverpelt family was robbed!" she breathed in surprise. The prominent family was the wealthiest in town and, as such, a natural target for thieves. According to the article, an unidentified creature snuck into the von Beaverpelts' palatial home one night and made off with a whole stash of jewels and silverware. The von Beaverpelts could give only a partial description of the intruder: skinny, long, and fast on its feet. A ferret or a weasel was suspected, or possibly a rat (assuming the witnesses didn't see the tail). No arrests were ever made.

"Huh." Vera pondered that. It made sense for a thief to try to rob such a tempting house, but what could it have to do with Julia? Even the slenderest moose would never be mistaken for a ferret!

Suddenly a shadow loomed across Vera's paper. She turned to see BW standing there. "You're blocking my light," she said, removing her glasses to polish.

"You're blocking my deadline, Vixen. Aren't you supposed to be working for me?"

"I am. I'm doing research for a story."

"Don't try to fool me! What are you up to?" BW asked. "Everything down here is literally old news. Old news doesn't sell papers."

Vera jabbed her paw into his pudgy chest. "Oh, it does when it links up with new news! Trust me on this, BW. When I'm done, everyone will want to read the story I uncover."

The skunk bared his teeth for a second, then said, "All right. You can dig around in this mausoleum for a little while. But don't you forget that Ms. Grey expects you to show up at a class or two, and I expect a pretty, tidy story on Shady Hollow's new business!"

"I'll get there, I promise."

Vera waited till BW bustled off. She had a whole list of new creatures to interview: The von Beaverpelts, for information on the robbery. Professor Heidegger, to ask if he saw anything the night Julia vanished. And, of course, Octavia Grey, her new instructor in manners.

First things first, though. Vera would find out more about the von Beaverpelt robbery and decide if Julia could have been involved somehow.

Chapter 13

Vera finished her careful perusal of the eleven-year-old papers and returned them neatly to the cart. Then she politely thanked the archivist and made her way back upstairs and into daylight. As she walked, she gathered her thoughts and put together a game plan. She knew Edith von Beaverpelt would be at home and that Stasia would most likely be there as well. Esme, of course, would be hard at work at Joe's Mug, pouring coffee with a smile.

Ah, coffee. Vera's mind wandered and reminded her that she'd had no coffee yet that morning. Silly librarians and their rules! Vera knew things would go better for everyone if she interviewed Esme first and scored a cup of coffee (or two) while doing it.

Vera made a quick stop at her desk to check for any messages and then went out to conduct her interviews. Finding none, she escaped the office before anyone could rope her into a favor or some off-topic task.

She enjoyed the brisk walk from the offices of the *Herald* to the coffee shop. It was a perfect autumn day. The sky was that deep blue that one sees only in the heart of fall, and the leaves were reaching their peak of color. The sun was shining, the air was crisp, and it was easy to forget there was evil in the world.

When Vera arrived at Joe's Mug, the morning rush was over, and Esme was the only waitress on duty. In fact, the café was mostly empty except for an elderly ferret who was reading the paper over a cup of tea. Vera nodded at the beast, called a good morning to Esme, and chose a table in the far corner of the diner.

When Esme approached the table to take her order, Vera requested a bowl of oatmeal with raisins and brown sugar and a large black coffee. Before Esme could go back to the kitchen, Vera put out her paw and touched the beaver lightly.

"Could I have a quick word with you while you're not too busy?" Vera asked. "It's about a robbery at your house quite a few years ago."

The beaver looked startled, not expecting to be asked about that. But she nodded.

"Let me put in your order and get your coffee first"—Esme knew Vera well—"and then I can sit down for a few minutes."

Vera was pleased to see the young beaver bustling back to her table in just a few minutes with two large mugs and a full pot of coffee. *Esme is really just aces at her job,* Vera thought. Who would have guessed that of a highborn von Beaverpelt?

Esme poured the coffee for Vera and herself and then took

a seat opposite the fox. Vera clutched her mug and took an appreciative sip. Now that Vera had some fuel in her system, she was ready to go. She opened her notebook to a fresh page and looked at Esme.

"There was a robbery at your home eleven years ago," she began. "You would have been quite young, but do you remember anything about it?"

Esme thought for a moment as she sipped from her mug of coffee. "I don't remember much about the robbery itself, but I do remember how mad Mama and Papa were. There was a silver tea set missing that had belonged to Grandmama, most of the silver from when Mama and Papa got married, and lots of Mama's jewels. She was especially upset about the loss of an emerald-pendant necklace that Papa gave her when they got engaged."

Vera scribbled furiously in her notebook in between large sips of coffee. She was amazed that Esme could recall so much, and said so.

"Well," Esme said wryly, "certain events are more memorable than others. I couldn't tell you what most of my birthday presents were from year to year, but that robbery was another matter. I couldn't sleep for a month afterward. Every creak in the house made Stasia and me jump."

"Did they ever catch the robber or recover the valuables?" Vera asked, pouring second cups of coffee for herself and Esme.

"No. Not a single thing turned up," Esme replied. "Mama was heartbroken over the loss of that necklace. It was engraved on the back, and it really meant a lot to her. The tea set was engraved, too, I think. Frankly I missed the tea set more, since I never got to wear the necklace." Esme finished her coffee and stood up. "I'm afraid that's all I remember, Vera. I should get back to work, and I'm sure your oatmeal is getting cold."

"Thanks so much, Esme," the reporter said, "I appreciate your time. This helps a lot."

Vera finished her cup of coffee and forced herself to eat all the oatmeal. She didn't really care for oatmeal but knew it was good for her, and after all, a creature can't live on coffee alone. She paid her bill, leaving a generous tip for Esme, and headed toward the von Beaverpelt mansion. She could try to make an appointment, but she feared that Edith von Beaverpelt would make up an excuse not to see her. Vera had annoyed Edith quite a bit during a previous investigation last summer. So Vera decided to take her chances and just ring the doorbell at the stately residence.

After Reginald von Beaverpelt had been murdered, his widow inherited all his business interests. Vera knew, however, that Edith left most of the day-to-day work to Howard Chitters, her late husband's former accountant. The diminutive but hardworking Howard had proven himself a capable manager at the sawmill, which was why Vera felt confident that she would find Edith at home on a weekday morning.

Vera was a little winded as she made her way up the extremely long and curving pathway that led to the von Beaverpelt estate in Maple Heights. But what a view! She looked back and saw the town center of Shady Hollow in the middle of the wide valley. The streets lay in tidy lines, and the millpond sparkled bright blue in the sun; the colorful treetops spread out across the landscape. Yes, here a creature really could feel on top of the world.

She caught her breath as she stood on the porch and rang the doorbell. A mouse answered the door; she was dressed in the somewhat old-fashioned uniform of a domestic servant. One of the many Chitters children, perhaps.

"Yes?" the mouse asked squeakily.

Vera stepped boldly over the threshold. "Vera Vixen to see Mrs. von Beaverpelt," she said briskly, hoping the timid mouse would think she had an appointment. "Shall I wait in the drawing room?"

The mouse hurried after her, trying to stop her, but Vera had a head start and longer legs. She opened the door to the drawing room and found Edith and her daughter Stasia both drinking coffee and still in their robes despite the advanced hour.

"Good morning, ladies!" Vera declared, though she suspected it was technically afternoon. "How nice to find you both at home. May I take a few moments of your time? I have some questions about an old story that I'm working on."

Without waiting for an answer from the startled beavers, Vera perched on the end of a damask sofa. The mouse had quite given up by this time and left the doorway where she had been dithering. Vera hoped the mouse wouldn't get in too much trouble for letting Vera into the house.

Edith von Beaverpelt's eyes were wide with dismay. "This is quite irregular, Miss Vixen!"

"Forgive me, but it really won't take long. Do you remember the night your home was robbed? About eleven years ago?"

"Why would you care about *that*?" Anastasia asked, obviously not expecting this topic. "And how did you know? You weren't here then."

"Esme filled me in on what she remembers," Vera went on, ignoring Stasia's outburst, "but I'd like to hear from both of you."

"How is that possibly relevant now?" Edith asked, though in a much less belligerent tone. "Has something been found? Have the police recovered something?"

"If that were true, Deputy Braun would be here asking questions," Stasia said shrewdly. "He wouldn't send Miss Vixen on an errand . . . not *anymore*." Stasia's expression turned smug and gloating as she looked at Vera.

Vera bit her tongue and jotted a note in her little book, reminding herself to discover something truly embarrassing about Anastasia and then drop it to Gladys one day. Stasia really was the evil sister.

"I'm here for a story for the paper," Vera said, trying to remain calm. "No items from the robbery were recovered, as far as I know. But what interests me is the thief. Did any of you get a glimpse of the creature who did it? Can you remember anything at all?"

"I saw him," Edith said in a low voice. "I haven't thought of that night for years, but now that you bring it up, it's like it happened yesterday."

"What precisely did you see, Mrs. von Beaverpelt? Please take your time," Vera said gently. She knew how to encourage a witness.

"It was very late one night. It was midsummer, and all the windows and vents were open. It was so hot. It had been hot all week; we were desperate for a breeze. I wasn't sleeping well for just that reason. At around two or three in the morning, I heard a rustling. At first I thought it was the wind or even rain on the leaves. But when I sat up in bed, I *saw* a shadow. Something that just didn't fit." Edith's expression looked hunted. Every creature of the forest, no matter how civilized, maintains a certain instinct when it comes to predator and prey.

Sounds, shadows . . . These are signs that the back of the mind pays attention to. When things *don't fit*, instinct takes over. Vera had no doubt that Edith was telling the truth.

"What was it? The shadow?"

"A creature," Edith said, shivering. "Some lanky, thin beast. Very dark—not because of the night, you know. I mean it had a deep brown or gray coat, but I couldn't see any stripes, though it might have had some. And when it moved through a little beam of moonlight from the window, I saw its eyes. Piercing. It had the sharpest teeth, you know. I remember that because it was smiling at me—"

"It?" Vera asked. "Before you said *he*. Your statement to the police said it was a he as well."

"Oh, yes." Edith nodded. "Such height and strength. He was carrying a big sack that must've been filled with the silver and jewels with one paw, just slung it over his shoulder. He seemed as if he was about to come at me, and I screamed. Reggie was sleeping right by me, and he woke up. That made the robber dash for the window and leap out, sack and all. We never saw him again, nor any of the things that were stolen."

"Why now?" Stasia asked Vera. Her mother's chilling account of the robber's appearance had knocked some of the wind from her sails. "Why ask about this now?"

"The robbery occurred very close to the time when Julia Elkin disappeared," Vera said. "I think there could be a link."

"Oh, my!" Edith gasped. "The robber must have been lurking in the woods around town, waiting for another chance to rob a house. He must have killed Julia the night she left Shady Hollow! How horrible."

"It's a possibility," Vera said. "You can understand why even the tiniest detail might help me track this creature down. You said *lanky*. What sort of beast might it have been?" A ferret or a stoat was an obvious choice. But a rat was a possibility—a big thin one. Or a squirrel?

"I think . . . a weasel," Edith said hesitantly. "I just didn't see enough."

"You said you remember the teeth. Were they close together, like a rat's, or farther apart? The eyes—how big were they compared to the rest of the face? How widely set? The length of the paw—short and round or elongated? Trust your instincts."

"Oh." Edith sighed. "I just can't be sure. I keep coming back to *weasel*."

"Then you're probably right." Vera flipped the cover back over her notebook. "Thank you. You've helped."

"You think Julia was murdered by the same individual?" Stasia asked.

"I'm not sure. All I know is that she was alive when she left her home and her body turned up in an orchard a decade later. Something terrible happened in a very short time, and everyone in Shady Hollow deserves to know what that was."

Chapter 14

Vera left the von Beaverpelt mansion, her mind swirling. The idea of the robber killing Julia was tempting to believe; it exonerated Joe, and it meant that no one in Shady Hollow was guilty of the crime. Yet . . . something *didn't fit*. What was it?

As always, Vera sought out Lenore with these questions. The raven listened very carefully to Vera's report, then sat a long time. Vera kept quiet, knowing that Lenore was a deep thinker. She tried not to fidget.

"No," Lenore said at last. "Let's remember the method, the personality of the victim, and the killer." Lenore was a devoted reader of mysteries and was now applying all her knowledge to the problem. "Julia was buried. Buried deep. Think about it.

A robber who's just passing through wouldn't care if a body turned up. If he killed Julia for whatever she was carrying with her, he'd have just taken it and gone on his way. But we know he didn't kill her for her suitcase, because *we* found it where it was hidden. Anyway, he wouldn't bother to conceal the crime."

"I knew something didn't fit!" Vera cried. "Thank you. The burial implies either a need to conceal or a feeling of regret or both. The robber wouldn't have had either of those impulses." Then Vera realized something else. "Lenore!"

"What?"

"Something else doesn't fit. We found Julia's suitcase in the eastern woods. That's nowhere near the orchard, and there's no reason to think a creature would have—or could have—dragged the body all the way to Cold Clay Orchards just to bury it. Julia didn't have the suitcase with her. Even if she planned to leave town that night, she still hadn't actually gone through with it at the time she was killed."

"So she must have gone to the orchard on purpose," Lenore concluded, "either to meet someone or to find something. In any case, she had a reason for being there, and if you find out that reason, you'll be closer to knowing who killed her."

"I'll figure it out." Vera nodded confidently.

"One thing, Vera," the raven warned.

"What's that?"

"Maybe let folks continue to think that the robber was the killer," Lenore advised her. "We found out how ugly it got when neighbors were eyeing each other after the murder of Otto Sumpf. We don't want that happening again."

"But what if the murderer *is* a resident? Someone living in Shady Hollow all this time?"

"Then all the more reason to make them think that you don't suspect anyone in town." The raven was a very clever bird. "It'll put them at ease. Then you can investigate with less worry that someone's going to try to silence you . . . like last time!"

"Oh, stop with that. It turned out all right," Vera said.

"Because I was there to see it and because Orville came to rescue you and carry you back home for medical treatment! Speaking of, how's Orville?" Lenore's eyes bored into Vera's.

"Er . . . we haven't really spoken lately."

"You should. You're stronger together. Solving the case will go faster if you combine your talents. And I want you to be happy," Lenore added softly.

"Thank you for that. I guess I should go talk to him. It's not anyone's fault, after all . . . other than Gladys's."

"There you go," Lenore said. "Go make up with your beau. You'll feel better."

"I will, though not immediately. I think I have to stop by Octavia's school to set up my classes for that silly story."

"The faster you get it done, the faster you never have to do it again."

Vera nodded, recognizing the sense in that. "I'm off. See you later!"

She left the bookshop feeling far more optimistic than she did going in. She had a new direction for her investigation and new hope for her relationship with Orville. Fighting was beneath them both, she decided.

But first she had to set up some class times with Octavia. Vera found the door to the etiquette school unlocked, so she opened it and went inside. There was no one at the front desk, but music was wafting from upstairs, where the bulk of the school was located. She proceeded up the stairs to the spacious room above and heard a laugh echo down the stairs along with the musical notes. Octavia was in a good mood, apparently.

The music grew louder—some sort of waltz coming from a record player, perhaps. Vera hummed along with the tune until she reached the doorway. There she stopped short in total shock.

Octavia the silver-coated mink was dancing . . . with none other than Orville! This was no class, either. The creatures were the only two in the large room, and they appeared to be having a wonderful time. Vera didn't even think Orville knew how to dance, let alone enjoyed it. And yet here he was, waltzing along with a pretty new face. Clearly he didn't feel a need to talk to Vera about the gossip column. He'd already moved on.

Vera retreated from the doorway and fled down to the street level. She couldn't have moved any faster if the place was on fire.

A mouse was at the reception desk now. "Oh, Miss Vixen!" she squeaked. "Did you want to sign up for your complimentary class?"

"No!" Vera declared as she dashed out the door. She didn't need a class from Octavia Grey! She needed to get as far from this whole town as possible.

Vera sped away from the Hollow blindly until she had to slow and catch her breath. Among the brilliant autumn leaves of the surrounding woods, she calmed down . . . slightly. After a few moments, she realized that she was not that far from Professor Heidegger's. It was already late afternoon. This time of year meant swift sunsets—the owl might already be stirring inside his lofty home.

Vera took a gulping breath. Her personal life might be a mess, but that didn't change the fact that she was the only one in town who was trying to solve Julia's murder. She would speak to Professor Heidegger. With luck, the nocturnal bird might be able to supply a clue.

Chapter 15

Vera made a point of putting what she had seen at the etiquette school behind her and focusing on her investigation. After all, there was nothing she could do about Orville and Ms. Grey. If he'd decided he liked slinky minks, then Vera was better off knowing now! She would work on solving Julia's murder and protecting the town from predators. Clearly the police were too busy fishing and dancing to focus on the crime problem in their jurisdiction.

She walked toward the large tree that housed Professor Heidegger. A rustle of wings caught her attention as a large owl settled on the ground in front of her. Professor Heidegger blinked solemnly and gave Vera a courtly bow.

"I was out for a quick flight, but I happened to hear a creature advancing to this specific locale and thought it might be important. Are you looking for me, Miss Vixen?" he asked, settling his feathers.

Vera started slightly, as one does when a large owl appears out of the sky, but she relaxed at the owl's greeting. She was actually fond of the pompous old professor.

"Why, yes, sir," she replied, adding the *sir* unconsciously. Heidegger always made her feel like she was still in school. "I have some questions about Julia. Julia Elkin, Joe's wife? The moose?"

The old owl looked confused for a moment, but then his expression changed.

"*Oh*," he said with dire emphasis. "The moose who disappeared. I never really knew her name. We don't get too many creatures of that size in town, so of course I remember her. She and Joe came to town at least a dozen years back. The summer of—"

"Yes," Vera answered quickly. Professor Heidegger had a prodigious memory, but he did tend to drone on. Vera tried to keep him on topic. "That Julia Elkin. During the final summer she was here, did you ever notice her wandering around the forest at night? Late, when most other creatures were sleeping?"

"Well," Professor Heidegger replied slowly, "I don't want you to get the impression that I spend all my waking hours watching my neighbors, but I did notice that moose wandering about quite late a few times. Joe was up with the sun to open the café, which meant he went to bed earlier, too. But his wife—now that's another story."

This was as close to gossip as the academic owl had ever come. Vera wanted to keep him talking.

"How did you know it was Julia," she asked respectfully, "and not Joe or some other large creature?"

The professor looked slightly annoyed that his recollections should be called into question.

"Of course it was her," he snapped impatiently. "She was smaller than her husband, and she always wore a silver locket around her neck. It glinted in the moonlight."

Vera was thrilled that the owl remembered so many details from such a long time ago. The locket was quite the identifier. But what had Julia been doing out at night after her family was asleep?

"Did you see where she went?" Vera continued her line of questioning. "Which direction was she heading?"

"That summer was so hot," the owl said, "and the air was so still—difficult to catch an updraft on nights like that—but yes, I do remember her going in the direction of Cold Clay Orchards one night, although I can't say if she actually went all the way there or if it was *the* night. This would have been the very start of August. School had not yet begun."

"Do you remember if she was wearing her locket that night?"

"Hmmmmm. Yes. It was a clear night with a bright full moon. The silver sparkled and caught my eye."

Vera was pleased that Professor Heidegger remembered as much as he did. She thanked him for his time and wished him a good evening. She wanted to get together with Lenore to try to put the pieces of the puzzle together.

Just as Vera was about to take her leave, the owl spoke again.

"There is one more thing, Miss Vixen," he said slowly, gathering his thoughts. "Julia Elkin was not the only strange creature whom I spotted wandering around the woods. By *strange*, I am of course referring to those animals who are not nocturnal, the ones who don't belong in the woods in the middle of the night."

Those who don't belong. Vera stopped and turned around, her eyes bright with interest.

"I remember that during that same hot summer," the owl continued, "I noticed an unfamiliar beast, not someone I knew, slinking around the forest. It happened more than once, or I would not have taken note of it."

Vera waited expectantly but said nothing. She did not want to interrupt the professor's train of thought.

"It might have been a ferret or a weasel, only slightly larger. A creature with dark fur and very sharp teeth. Not anyone whom I had ever seen before. Whether it is significant, I can't say, but I didn't see the creature come autumn. It had moved on."

Now, here was a real clue! Vera thanked the professor again for his time and tried to keep her excitement in check. She really had to talk to Lenore.

Vera trotted back to town, eager to share her news and add it to what she'd already learned about the murder. This mysterious weasel creature—if that's what it was—*must* have had some connection to Julia. If Vera could locate any more information about the creature, such as where it lived while in the area, she might have enough evidence to definitively clear Joe of any blame. In fact, Vera was so intent on this new development that she didn't see Orville and nearly ran into him. She skidded to a halt, small clouds of dust billowing up on the track under her paws.

"Hello, Vera," Orville said. He smiled as if happy to see her.

Vera almost smiled back but then remembered just who he'd been dancing with earlier. She kept her voice level and her expression cool. "Oh, good evening, Orville. You'll have to excuse me. I really need to dash . . ."

"Dash where? Working on a story?"

"Yes!" Vera turned to head down Main Street but was dismayed when Orville simply ambled along beside her. "Er . . . I really am in a hurry."

"That's why I'm walking with you," he explained. "Don't want to slow you down. Where are you going?"

"Home. I have to compile my notes before I go."

"Go where?"

"Um . . . out. Tonight." *Oof.* She shouldn't have said that.

"Out where?" Orville asked. This time his tone wasn't Orville-being-friendly; it was Orville-being-a-deputy. "It's practically dark already."

"Yes. Well. I need to find something and it really can't wait."

"Where is it?"

"Um . . . the woods," she mumbled.

"You don't have a very good track record when it comes to going into the woods at night, Vera," Orville said. "I hope you're not going to do something foolish."

"Of course not! And I'll take Lenore."

"Lenore has a reading at the bookstore tonight—that Bradley Marvel writer." Orville was always pretty well apprised of what was going on around town. "So I don't think she can leave. Why not have dinner with me, and you can wander off into the woods tomorrow?"

"I'm not having dinner with you!"

"Why not? You've been running around all day. Aren't you hungry?"

"I don't have any food at home," she said, desperate for an excuse.

"No problem, we can go to the Bamboo Patch. My treat."

There were few things Vera liked more than the evening special at the Bamboo Patch, but she couldn't stand the idea of chitchatting with Orville, knowing he was already romancing someone else. So much for being new in town! "I can't do that," she said. "I should go to the bookstore."

"You just said you were going home."

"Yes, but I really should go to the reading. Can't believe I forgot about it! Lenore's such a good friend, and she supports my work. I should support hers!"

"Well, of course, I guess," Orville said, sounding a bit sad. "I just thought we could talk . . ."

"Another time, I'm afraid." Vera turned, for the bookshop was at the other end of the street.

Orville mimicked her move. "I'll walk you there, then."

"Oh, no need," she said. "It's not as if there's a murderer on the loose."

"I don't mind. I haven't seen much of you lately."

"Since Gladys wrote that article, you mean."

"It was pretty silly," he said. "I guess she wanted some attention for her gossip column, and anything would do. The only gossip folks seem to want to trade this week is old . . . all about Julia Elkin."

Despite everything, Vera glanced over at him. "What are they saying?"

"Oh, the usual. Thing is, everyone kind of knew that Julia

and Joe didn't get on too well. So what else can we say? I was telling Ms. Grey all about it today."

"Oh, really?"

"Yes. She asked about the whole business. I think she was concerned that she picked the wrong town to set up shop. But I told her that Shady Hollow is quite safe . . . usually. And that if something happens, Vera Vixen will get to the bottom of it."

"You told her that?"

"Naturally. She seems quite impressed with you. Asked all sorts of questions."

"So you talked with her?"

"Um, yes. A bit." Orville looked away—guiltily, to Vera's mind. "Well, we're at the bookstore. See you later." He managed to leave the vicinity very fast.

Vera sighed and went into the store. She had attended such events before, but her schedule made it difficult to consistently show the support that Lenore's shop deserved. Happily, plenty of other folks from the Hollow were there as well. Everyone was excited to hear about the latest thriller from the acclaimed Bradley Marvel.

When Vera got into the bookstore, she immediately looked around for Lenore. The raven was flapping around the front window, directing some of her booksellers to change the signs. She seemed nervous and distracted—not her usual calm self.

"Hey, Lenore." Vera drew her friend's attention. "What's going on? Can I help?"

"Oh, Vera!" replied the distraught bookstore proprietor. "We had a last-minute cancellation, and I've had to come up with a replacement speaker. Bradley Marvel was supposed to be here tonight."

"Yes! I was just looking at one of his books the other day."

"You and a bunch of others. Folks were really excited. I've been advertising for weeks!"

Vera vaguely remembered seeing posters all over town depicting a dangerous-looking wolf in a fedora. She had been interested in going to the event, having read a few of Marvel's books over the years. But the discovery of the bones had distracted her.

"Well," Lenore went on, moving a stack of shiny thrillers by Marvel and replacing them with some slender paperbacks featuring a ship on the covers, "apparently Bradley Marvel is the victim of a terrible flu and was forced to cancel most of his tour. I had to get a replacement at the last minute. I would have just done without an event tonight, but I already ordered hors d'oeuvres and wine and I don't want them to go to waste."

Vera realized that this amounted to a professional disaster for her friend. The bookshop operated on a careful budget, and Lenore did not often have food and drink at author events. This time, she had gone all out on the popular author, planning to recoup the money she spent in book sales.

"So who is coming instead?" Vera asked, almost afraid to hear the answer. Anyone who was available at the last minute couldn't be nearly as well known or successful.

From the expression on Lenore's face, the raven knew this as well. "Wilbur Montague was free," she said quietly.

Vera groaned inwardly. Wilbur Montague was a writer and a historian who lived a few towns away from Shady Hollow. A slovenly boar who always smelled strongly of cigars, he would talk to any creature about his work for hours on end if they stood still long enough. His area of expertise was shipwrecks, but really he seemed to be an expert in almost everything. At least, he seemed to think so.

This had the makings of a fiasco. Folks would be extremely disappointed not to meet Bradley Marvel. They would be even more upset to learn that he was being replaced by Wilbur Montague, boar and bore. At least there would be food and drink. That would help for a while, but half the audience would leave after they ate and drank, and they certainly wouldn't buy a dull academic tome on shipwrecks when they'd been counting on picking up the latest Marvel thriller. Vera couldn't think of anything helpful to say, so she decided to browse the shop before the event started, determined to buy as many books as she could afford.

As Vera moved through the biography section at the front of the store, her eye caught on a display: an oversize book whose cover featured a regal-looking dark-furred mink wearing an elaborate crown. Interesting. It put her in mind of Octavia, naturally, and Vera put the book in her basket, thinking that some research on the new mink in town couldn't hurt. After all, how many aristocratic mink dynasties could there be? Perhaps she'd even get some background on Octavia's bloodline or find something she could use to discourage Orville from dancing with her every day. Maybe the Greys were locked in an ancestral battle with a bear clan or something . . . There was always hope. Vera took a deep breath, realizing that she was still thinking of Orville and Octavia. *Stop it!* she told herself. There were other things to worry about.

Vera continued to browse. Shady Hollow was certainly fortunate to have such a terrific store. Lenore worked day and night, bringing in authors to speak and ordering the latest books from the city, whether thrillers or award-winning literary fiction. Lenore was often the first creature at the docks on the days the barge came upriver with all the items folks around town had ordered. She saw to it that all her books arrived safely. When she wasn't at work, she was reading, reading, reading. She was always willing to talk about the latest novel from an established author or the first effort by a writer who was just starting out. Along with books, the store also displayed charming bookmarks and other little gifts. And, of course, mugs. Lenore knew her readers.

Folding chairs had been set up on the ground floor where the readings were held. Unfortunately, many of the attendees left when they learned that Bradley Marvel was a no-show (not before helping themselves to a cup of wine and a miniature quiche, though; free food and drink are always a draw). Vera took a glass of wine and nodded at a few of her neighbors. She really hoped she could stay awake for the presentation. She would love to get started on her investigation in the woods, but she could not abandon Lenore in her hour of need. The raven needed moral as well as financial support.

Vera took a seat near the back. It was almost time for the reading to begin.

Lenore perched on the lectern and welcomed everyone to Nevermore Books. "Thank you so much for coming," she said, addressing the group, which was much smaller than she had hoped. "I know you were looking forward to seeing Bradley Marvel, but unfortunately he is too ill to travel. However, we were lucky enough to get a replacement whom many of you may be familiar with. Here to talk about his latest book, *Lost to the Briny Deep*, please welcome Wilbur Montague."

The boar shuffled up to the podium. He was carrying a

messy sheaf of papers. Vera could smell stale cigar smoke from where she sat. She was afraid it would be quite late before she could leave the reading. She could tell that Wilbur would not give up his captive audience easily. It even seemed like some audience members were holding on to hope that Bradley Marvel would appear. Alas for them.

As the author droned on about shipwrecks and the history of boatbuilding, Vera let her mind wander to her case. What had Julia and her friend been planning? Where did they meet? Was there any creature still in town who knew anything about the moose who disappeared?

Finally, after what seemed like hours but was really only forty-five minutes, Lenore cut the boar off mid-ramble.

"That's all the time we have! Everyone, thanks so much for coming," she twittered. "Mr. Montague's book is for sale at the front desk, and he will be happy to sign it for you and answer any questions you may have for him. Have a wonderful evening." The scattered applause seemed to assuage the boar.

Because she had been sitting in the back, Vera managed to beat the crowd to the register.

"Thank you for staying all the way through," Lenore breathed as she rang up Vera's purchase.

"Happy to help," Vera whispered back. She paid for the book on minks and a few other items. "I've got some news on the investigation. I'll fill you in tomorrow." Then she gratefully made her escape onto the street while Lenore tended to the next customer.

It was too late to search the woods. Actually, Vera was looking forward to heading back to her den and curling up to sleep, since it had been a long and emotional day. She would put the kettle on, brew up her favorite nighttime chamomile-and-lavender tea, maybe page through her new books, and not think about Orville . . . not even once . . .

"Oh, Miss Vixen," a voice called from a little ways up the street.

Vera snapped out of her musings to see none other than Octavia waving to her with one elegant paw. There was no way for Vera to evade this without embarrassing herself, so she forced a smile.

"Hello, Ms. Grey. I didn't see you there." Vera stopped a few feet away from where Octavia was standing on the corner.

"I'm so glad I caught you, Vera. And none of that 'Ms. Grey' business. One wishes to call one's friends by name, and I do hope we will be dear friends."

"Why . . . sure." Vera had been about to say something quite different, but it wasn't the time to bring up the awkward fact that friends typically did not romance the beaux of other friends.

"I was thinking," Octavia went on, blithely unaware of Vera's mental state, "of what class of mine you might most enjoy as you prepare for the newspaper article. At first, I wanted you to join the ballroom dance . . ."

Vera's expression must have warned her.

"But then I thought public speaking and diplomacy would better suit you. I know you'll one day be so famous that you'll be giving speeches and accepting awards left and right!" Octavia beamed happily at Vera. "How does that sound? It's an advanced class, of course, but you'll have no difficulty. Tomorrow at five p.m.?"

"Uh, sure."

"Never *uh*, dear," Octavia lectured gently. "A pause is acceptable if you must frame your answer."

"Will do. Thanks. Got to go!" Vera sped away as fast as her legs could carry her. Diplomacy? What sort of folks did Octavia think lived in Shady Hollow? No one around here was joining diplomatic missions to foreign governments. The closest thing Shady Hollow had to that was Sun Li, who had emigrated from the east to embark on a new career. And his diplomacy was all done on the stove!

Vera sighed in relief once she reached her home. Somewhat unusually, she locked the door, vowing that no one would disturb her until tomorrow morning at the earliest. She was tired, but she didn't sleep well. Instead she dreamed of pathless woods and strange shadowy creatures just at the edge of her vision.

When the sun rose, Vera was grateful. It would be far better to search for the long-ago robber's hideout in the daytime. Vera headed outside almost immediately, not wanting to lose time. Since she had very little food at home, she stopped at Joe's Mug.

Joe Junior was behind the counter when Vera walked in. "Morning, Miss Vixen," he said, polite as always. "What'll it be? Besides coffee, I mean."

"How about a slice of that pumpkin pie?" Vera pointed to a particularly luscious-looking pie in the display case. She strongly believed in pie for breakfast.

"Sure thing. Add whipped cream?"

Vera just narrowed her eyes at him.

Joe Junior chuckled, sounding remarkably like his father. "I figured. Just wanted to make sure you aren't some impostor!"

Vera sat at the counter and was soon devouring warm pie

accented with a billowy cloud of whipped cream. The coffee was fresh and strong and gave Vera the feeling that she could accomplish anything today.

"Where's Esme?" she asked, looking around. It was still early, so perhaps the beaver hadn't arrived to work yet.

"She's in the office, trying to learn proper bookkeeping," Joe Junior said. "She's *very* good with numbers," he added. "Lucky, 'cause I'm sure not."

"She'll pick it up like it's nothing. But if she's got questions, Howard Chitters can help."

"He's so busy nowadays," Joe Junior said, referring to the fact that, following the untimely death of his employer, the once-put-upon mouse now essentially ran the sawmill, which was Shady Hollow's biggest business. "We shouldn't bother him with a little problem."

Vera caught something in Joe Junior's tone. "Wait. *Is* there a problem?"

"Well, we're not sure. Esme was looking through the old ledgers to see how to do things, and she ran across some . . . mistakes."

The reporter in Vera suddenly got very interested in this development—but then half a dozen creatures entered the diner, all eager for prework breakfast. "Okay, Joe," she said. "You get to work . . . but I want to talk about this later!"

He nodded and moved off to serve the sudden rush.

Vera licked her plate clean—she was no fool—and left her payment on the counter. *Time to put that pie and coffee to good use.* She headed out of town, toward the woods where Professor Heidegger said he'd seen a mysterious creature moving around so long ago.

On this fine autumn morning, the woods were beautiful

and peaceful. Sunlight filtered through the changing leaves, and a light breeze sent some of those leaves wafting slowly down to the ground, where they carpeted the forest floor in blazing yellows, oranges, and vibrant reds.

Vera's paws crunched on the layer of dried leaves, and she enjoyed the mingled scents of pine and soil. As she walked, she looked for potential places where a creature might set up a temporary home. For all their beauty, the woods weren't quite ideal for most folk, who preferred the conveniences and assets of living in civilization. What would a creature avoiding those things need? Shelter from wind and rain. A lookout, probably. And water.

The fox sniffed carefully. She knew a stream ran through these woods, and she thought she detected a faint smell of water. She walked several paces north, then pricked her ears. Yes, there was the rushing of water. She kept onward, until she ran into the bank of a little stream.

"This must run into the millpond eventually," Vera muttered as she looked along the bank. She had to choose to go left—back toward town—or right—farther into the woods. She chose to go right, reasoning that any thief who chose to hide in the woods in the first place wouldn't balk at hiding *deep* in the woods.

She continued to follow the bank, casting her gaze all around as she went. The robber would want to stay fairly close to the stream, which was the only source of water in the area. Vera walked for a little while and then, where the land started to rise a bit on either side of the stream, she noticed a patch of darkness in a hillside.

Vera scrambled up from the bank. The hill was rocky and rough, and underneath one of the large ledges was an opening to some sort of cave. When she reached it, Vera looked into the darkness. There was no hint of the cave's end, and there was no sound from within.

"Halloooo?" Vera called softly. No one answered; there wasn't even an echo.

She edged her way into the cave. The light coming from the entrance failed rapidly as she moved farther inside, but her vision was sharp and she wasn't afraid. The cave appeared to go back quite some way, the floor sloping as the cave descended into the earth. But whoever lived here hadn't gone that far. Vera saw several items left behind: a tin pot, a big rusty spoon, and a pile of matted and rotten fluff that was likely the ruins of some bedding. She'd found somebody's abandoned camp. But was it the robber's?

She rooted around, focusing on the detritus of the little camping area. Whoever it was had left in a hurry because an itinerant creature would pack everything up to move to the next camp. Some creatures were transient—they had no permanent home but instead wandered from place to place on a migration that never ended.

Vera sighed unhappily. Was this a real lead? She had no evidence that it was the robber who stayed here and not an ordinary hermit. Even if he had, what good would it do her to know that? In frustration, she kicked a small pile of leaves and old grass.

As she did, something glimmered faintly, then disappeared. Vera tipped her head, trying to catch the reflection again. Once, twice . . . there it was!

She put a paw over the little gleam and felt a hard pebble. Picking up the object, Vera was amazed to discover a small yet beautiful stone. She moved into the stronger light at the entrance. There she was dazzled by the deep green color of the stone she held. An emerald, surely! This place *had* to be the robber's old lair, and this stone had been lost somehow, separated from the haul.

Revived by the discovery, Vera turned back inside. If the robber had left this behind, he might have left something else behind as well . . . something she could use to learn about him or to trace his whereabouts.

She looked everything over very carefully, even poking through the remains of the bedding (which revealed only a lot of skittering bugs that made Vera yelp in surprise). The big rusty spoon had something written on the handle, but it was worn to nearly nothing. She put the spoon in her bag, intending to decipher the words later. The pot also had something on the bottom—an imprint from the factory that made it. Vera squinted, trying to read the half-eroded words.

CRA TH PRI NOR ND OOK Y CO.

She puzzled it out slowly. "'Crafted . . . with . . . pride . . . Northland Cookery Company!'" Well, that put coincidence out the door. The robber had lived here, and he must have had contact with Julia Elkin before her death. Joe's family was from much farther north, and it was very unlikely that an item from a small local business would get all the way south to Shady Hollow by coincidence. Contrarily, it would have been natural for Joe to order items from a trusted company when setting up his diner. So the pot had probably come from Joe's supply and had possibly been stolen, but it more likely was given to the robber from Julia herself. Why? For charity? Or had the robber threatened her? Had Julia been running from not Joe but perhaps another danger?

Vera didn't know—yet. But she would find out. Satisfied that she had something to go on, Vera snatched up the pot and left the cave, emerging into the bright autumn sunlight. She blinked as her eyes adjusted.

Her stomach growled suddenly. That piece of pumpkin pie must have worn off.

Chapter 16

Vera really wanted to talk to Lenore about her find in the woods, but as she was quite hungry and wanted to question Joe Junior and Esme about the odd accounting issues, she elected to return to the café for lunch and to try to learn more before she shared the results of her investigation with Lenore.

Joe's Mug was quite a bit more crowded than when Vera stopped in for coffee and pie earlier. She noted that Esme was waiting tables in half the diner and the mink Lucy was dealing with the counter. Vera chose an empty table in a corner. As she looked over the menu, she saw the special was tomato soup with a grilled cheese sandwich. This seemed perfect, as she felt a little chilled from her sojourn in the woods.

"How are you doing, Vera?" Esme asked, standing next to the fox with her order pad ready.

"Nice to see you, Esme," Vera replied. "I'll have the special and a cup of mint tea. When things slow down for you, I have a few more questions."

Esme glanced around as if estimating how much time it would take to serve all the creatures crowding the café.

"It might take a while," she said, "but as soon as I'm free, I'll stop by your table."

Vera thanked her and settled back in her chair to peruse the crowd and think about her find in the woods.

After the hardworking reporter finished her delicately herbed tomato soup and grilled cheddar on sourdough, she sipped a second cup of tea and waited for the young beaver waitress to sit down with her at the table. The lunch rush was winding down since folks had to get back to work.

Esme headed to Vera's table and sat down with an audible sigh of relief.

"Waiting tables is hard work," Vera noted.

"Sure, but it certainly beats lying around the mansion with Mother and Stasia." Esme looked around the café. "Turns out I like to keep busy."

Vera happened to know that Esme was also proud of herself for contributing to the family's finances. This trait made her the complete opposite of her sister, Stasia, who liked nothing better than depleting the family's fortune, usually by shopping or going to expensive places.

"How's the bookkeeping coming along?" Vera asked as Esme sipped a cup of coffee.

"Not too bad," the beaver replied. "I'm learning a lot from looking at the old account books, and I'm thinking about taking an accounting course at the community college. That would really send Mama over the edge."

This remark made Vera smile as she thought about Edith von Beaverpelt. Not only was Edith's daughter working a menial job, but she planned on attending a community college, too? Vera admired Esme for her ambition but knew that Edith wanted to marry off both her daughters as soon as possible.

"I think that's terrific," Vera said. "I'm sure that Joe appreciates the help."

Esme looked around the café and then leaned forward to Vera. "His wife used to do the books, you know," she confided, "and Joe has just sort of done the best he can since she left. But he's not as tidy when it comes to the accounts."

"Esme," Vera prodded, "did you notice any irregularities in the diner's accounts? Anything out of the ordinary?"

Esme glanced around once more and answered Vera in a low tone, "I looked at the accounts from the year Julia, you know, disappeared. Just out of curiosity."

Vera nodded encouragingly, her stomach starting to clench with anticipation.

"There was an enormous sum of money missing the month Julia disappeared." Esme confirmed Vera's suspicions. "The entry was marked *Withdrawal—personal*. No other details. As far as I can tell, the money was never returned to the business."

"Did you ask Joe about it?" Vera asked.

"I was going to," Esme answered, "but then the body turned up and Orville took Joe in for questioning. I was afraid to mention it because the police might get the wrong idea. Orville might think Joe hired a killer to get rid of his wife and that the sum was a payout."

"You've been reading too many Bradley Marvel books,"

Vera chided the young beaver. "You know that Joe would never do such a thing."

"*I* know that," said Esme, "but it could look really bad if someone is being lazy and just wants an easy theory. You know those police bears don't know what they're doing." As soon as this came out of her mouth, Esme must have remembered who she was talking to, because she looked embarrassed. "Sorry."

"Don't worry about it," Vera answered serenely. "I've often thought the same. Why do you suppose I'm conducting my own investigation?"

"So it *is* an investigation, after all," said a new voice. The elder Joe had come up to the booth. He'd been surprisingly silent for all his bulk.

"Joe!" said Vera and Esme at the same time. "You're back!"

"Mr. Fallow secured my release," Joe explained. "I'm not out of the woods yet, but he argued, very convincingly, that I was not a flight risk and that the business could suffer irreparable harm should I be kept away unnecessarily. And he said that if I were found innocent—"

"And you will be!" Vera interjected.

"—it would open the police up to a civil case. Don't know if I believe that, but the important thing is that Chief Meade did. So I'm allowed to be out and about. I have to check in at the station twice a day."

"That's a relief," Esme said. "I already called Lucy and told her to come in for some extra shifts since I didn't know when you'd be here."

"Keep her on the schedule," Joe said. "No telling when I might be back in a cell. Vera, what's this you're asking about money?"

"Hey, Joe," Vera said. "It's an investigation, but you're not a suspect. Not to me. You know I'm not trying to bring up old hurts for nothing, but I've got to find out what happened to Julia. You heard what we were talking about just now, didn't you? What's the story?"

Joe sighed. "The missing money? Not much of a story, I'm afraid. Julia took it right before she left, and I didn't realize it till the next month when I had to pay the regular bills."

"You didn't report it to the police?" Vera asked, already knowing the answer.

"No." Joe shook his head. "I couldn't. I kept hoping Julia would come back, see? And how could she pick up life here again if there was a report of missing money? So I kept quiet."

"Joe, you should have reported it! Then there would be some proof of your side of the story."

"I never thought . . ." The moose looked ashamed.

Vera sighed. "Never mind, Joe. How could you have known?"

Esme, who had been sitting there in silence, finally spoke up. "It's too bad you never got the money back, Joe. It was a lot."

"I managed," Joe said. He lowered his voice. "I had to dip into the savings we'd started for Joe Junior. He was young! Too young to need it yet. And I paid it all back. Took a few years, but I added extra to his account every chance I could."

"And that's why the café's books never showed the discrepancy; you were using a different account," Vera concluded. "Don't worry, this detail won't make it into any story I write." She was a reporter, not a hack.

"Thanks, Vera." Joe shuffled off to the kitchen.

Vera thanked Esme for her help and then went over to the counter to pay her check.

"That was amazing, as always, Joe," Vera complimented the young moose. "You certainly inherited your father's culinary skills."

Joe Junior looked embarrassed but pleased as he took her money and gave her the change.

Vera continued the conversation, as there was no one waiting in line behind her. "Say, Joe," she went on, "what is the name of the cookware business your dad used when he set up? The one up north?"

"Northland Cookery Company," replied Joe Junior. "Clever, huh? I have no idea how they came up with it." He chuckled.

At this, Vera decided she had asked enough questions for the day and, after she thanked Joe Junior again, she took her leave.

Vera had barely left Joe's Mug when she remembered the emerald that she found in the cave. She hurried back into the café and spotted Esme wiping down tables.

"I forgot one thing," she called out. "What do you make of this?" she asked Esme, fishing the stone out of her bag.

The beaver took one look at the gleaming jewel and pronounced, "Fake." Then she went back to wiping tables.

Vera couldn't believe it. She was sure she had discovered a real emerald! "How do you know?" she asked, her eyes narrowing.

"Trust me, I can spot the difference. Mama has plenty of costume jewelry," Esme answered. "*Some* of it's real, naturally. She has a few good pieces that Papa bought her. She's always kept those items in a vault in the cellar. But most of it—the sparkly things you see her wear to board meetings and charity luncheons and whatnot—is almost all fake. She knows most creatures can't tell the difference. Um, no offense, Vera."

Vera had to admit that she certainly had been fooled. What did she know about jewels, anyway? "I guess you learn something every day. I thought I'd hit the jackpot and found a clue at the same time."

"It's a clue? Where'd you find it?"

"In a cave outside town. I suspected that the robber who invaded your home all those years ago hid out there. This was going to be my proof," Vera added sadly.

"Well, it still is," Esme said. "That robber stole a lot of things, but he never got into the vault. Didn't Mama mention that? The only reason he got the real emerald necklace was because Mama wore it to a party and then left it on her dressing table that night instead of locking it up right away. Besides that, the robber got only the silver and some pretty little knick-knacks, and the stuff from Mama's jewel case—"

"The fake stuff!" Vera said, enlightened. "He must have been furious later. He probably thought he'd committed his last crime, that he was set for life. And instead—"

"He ended up with just a bunch of cut glass," Esme said with a firm nod. "Serves him right, I say. Still miss that tea set, though," she added more wistfully. "It *was* real silver, and we loved it. It was so pretty, with all these etched roses and butter-flies. When Mama pulled it out, we knew it was a *special* occasion. Oh, well."

"He would have sold it," Vera said. "He had to make money somehow, since those fake jewels weren't going to help. Thanks, Esme. You've been so helpful."

The beaver nodded. "Anytime."

After Vera left the café, she sauntered in a loop through town on her way back to the newspaper office. She took her time, enjoying the sunshine and the colors of the changing leaves. Autumn really was her favorite time of year. She was mulling over what she had just learned from Esme and Joe when she caught sight of a creature exiting the local pub. The gray fur, black stripes, and masked eyes were unmistakable.

"Hey there, Lefty!" she called out, thinking she had a number of questions to ask the raccoon.

Lefty whirled around at the sound of his name and, instead of responding, took off down the street in the opposite direction. For a moment, Vera just stood there, staring after the fleeing raccoon. Then she spurred into action.

Chapter 17

Vera began to chase Lefty down the street, convinced that he must be guilty of *something* if he was so quick to try to avoid her. She followed the path Lefty had used, ignoring the stares from a few creatures nearby as she zoomed past.

"Excuse me!" she barked out. "Reporter coming through!"

Maybe it wasn't polite, but Vera did not care. She was investigating a murder, and she was pretty sure the raccoon knew something. As soon as Vera had learned about the robbery at the von Beaverpelt mansion, she suspected that Lefty had to be involved on some level. He was a notorious petty criminal. If a creature was trying to move stolen goods in Shady Hollow, especially jewels, then Lefty was the beast to meet.

The chase continued, but Lefty was getting out of her sight.

She couldn't speculate about her case *and* chase a suspect. "Priorities, Vera!" she yelled at herself.

She put her head down and doubled her speed. She caught up to the raccoon by the bank of the river. Unless he wanted to swim, there was nowhere for him to go. "Lefty, hold up!" Vera stopped and panted, trying to catch her breath after the absurd race across town. Who knew what would show up in Gladys's gossip column about that? Maybe "Jilted Fox Chases New Beau!"

Vera put it out of her mind and turned to face her quarry, who was also recovering his breath, his little paws on his heaving belly.

"Lefty, what's the matter with you? I just wanted to ask you a few questions. Why did you run?"

"I didn't see that it was you, Vera!" the raccoon answered, looking as sheepish as it was possible for one of his species to look. "I thought you were Orville trying to pin something on me! But I've been clean for months!"

"Months?"

"Weeks, then," he amended hastily. "I'm turning over a new leaf. That's what I told Rhonda. She's been after me to get a real job. She thinks I ought to settle down." Rhonda was Lefty's partner—in crime and in life.

Vera wanted to laugh, but she controlled herself. She glanced past Lefty to the river, which rushed along, its waters running smooth and deep and wetting the bank into a muddy sheen. The river was a vital part of the town's economy, both legal and illegal. There were many little boathouses and docks along its banks, and some opened for business only when the law was looking the other way. If Lefty was down here, he was probably up to no good. Still, that wasn't Vera's business.

"I have a few questions for you about some missing jewels," she began, "from around the time Julia Elkin disappeared."

"That's a real long time ago," he hedged.

"I bet you can remember." Vera gave him a look letting him know that she was going to be persistent about this.

"You know I don't like to talk shop," Lefty replied finally. "But I guess it can't hurt now. The truth is, I came on a whole bag of loot a day or two after the robbery. It had been tossed on the side of the road."

"Which road?"

"The south track, the one that leads to . . . Cold Clay Orchards." Lefty's eyes widened. "Oh, dear."

"What were the valuables?" Vera asked.

"Jewels. Some loose, some set in rings and necklaces. I heard that the von Beaverpelt mansion got hit, and of course everyone was looking at *me*. But until I saw those jewels, I didn't have a thing to do with the robbery. Promise!"

Vera wanted to ask more questions, but she held her tongue while the raccoon was talking. She didn't want to interrupt and cause him to clam up altogether.

"So," Lefty continued, "I took the jewels down to my contact—and no, I ain't giving anything up about who that was! It doesn't matter anyway because he didn't buy anything I had. At first he was mad, and then he just laughed at me. The jewels were completely worthless. Turns out they were made out of glass or paste—total fakes."

"Your score was a little too good to be true," Vera said. "What did you do with it?"

"Nothing," said Lefty, with a sigh. "I had a pile of glass pebbles on my paws and no customers for them. I hid them and just waited for the whole robbery business to blow over. To be honest, I forgot all about it until this week, when the body was found."

"And no one in town mentioned missing jewels to you? Or a sack of loot? Or brought up any strangers in the area?"

Lefty just shook his head. "Got to understand, fox. The sort of business I'm in . . . there's no questions. That way we all know just as much as we need to."

"Thanks, Lefty." Vera knew she wouldn't get anything else out of the raccoon. She was pretty sure he only talked as much as he had because he had been enjoying an afternoon drink when she spotted him in town. She turned to walk back to the newspaper office but then thought of something.

"What'd you do with the fakes?" Vera asked. "Are they still hidden?"

"No. A few years ago, I gave them to the school, when the senior class put on that production of *The Pirate Queen*. They needed props for the set."

Vera nodded. How like Lefty. He was ready to run at any moment, yet he donated to the school play!

Vera had hoped to check in with Lenore to talk over all that she had learned, but she caught sight of the large clock in the town square and noted that it was already after four.

"Bother," Vera mumbled to herself. She had an etiquette lesson with Octavia as part of the story series the mink and the skunk had cooked up for her. She would love to skip it, but it was for the paper, and she was pretty certain that she'd get in major trouble if she didn't finish at least one article soon.

Instead of stopping at Nevermore Books like she wanted, Vera turned onto Elm Street and headed for Grey's School of Etiquette. She really did not want to waste an afternoon chatting with the very creature Orville was now dancing with. But perhaps she would learn something useful.

Inside the school, Vera had barely any time to look around before Octavia silently glided out from her office, elegant as ever, her silver fur gleaming softly in the late-afternoon light.

"Why, Vera," she purred, "how absolutely lovely to see you again. Are you ready for our lesson?"

Vera wanted to shrug, but she figured that she could give as good as she got. "Oh, Octavia," she answered in a voice that she did not recognize as her own. "It's wonderful to see you as well. I have been looking forward to this all day."

The mink looked a trifle surprised but recovered nicely. "Wonderful. I thought we'd begin with a formal tea, since so many important discussions occur in such settings."

She led Vera upstairs and into the large space on the second floor. Set up in the exact middle of the wide area cleared for dancing was an elaborate tea service on a table between two chairs. A long starched tablecloth fell to the floor, and tall taper candles burned, lighting the table. The whole scene looked very dramatic.

Vera took it all in. There was an ornate tea tray with a large silver teapot, a creamer pitcher, and a sugar bowl. Delicate china cups and saucers with matching plates were laid at each place. It was all extremely fussy and proper—and unexpected for Vera, who thought she'd merely have to speak standing up.

Still, the fox decided to play along. She seated herself on one side of the tea table, oohing and aahing over the silver and the dishes. There was also a three-tiered stand with scones, tiny frosted cakes, and miniature fruit tarts. Now that was some etiquette she could endorse! Vera snatched a tart and popped it into her mouth. The flavor of cranberry burst on her tongue, but Octavia's disapproving look took some of the enjoyment out of the treat.

"Sorry," Vera mumbled after wiping the crumbs from her snout. "It just looked so good."

"I understand, dear. But next time, do remember to wait until the dish is passed. I will pour the tea first."

It was not until Octavia picked up the fancy teapot to pour the tea that Vera really looked at the vessel. She had been too dazzled by the whole setup to notice many details. But now she took a long look at the teapot as the mink poured tea into Vera's cup. It was real silver, with a delicate design of roses and butterflies. Esme's description came back to Vera. Could this be the very same teapot that was stolen from Edith von Beaverpelt so long ago?

Vera pulled her gaze away from the teapot and focused on the display of tasty goodies. She didn't want to explain her interest in the teapot, and she certainly didn't want it to disappear before she had a chance to examine it closer and test out a theory or two.

She chewed thoughtfully on a blueberry scone as the mink poured her own tea. Vera added two tiny lumps of sugar to her cup and stirred carefully with a small silver spoon. The sugar bowl was also silver, but it didn't match the set; it was far more modern in design. Vera wondered at the anomaly but didn't have much time to think it over. The scones awaited!

While engaging in small talk, she tried to act as if she had meals like this every day. She was much more accustomed to eating takeout from the Bamboo Patch at her desk, but that was her own business. If only BW hadn't decided that Vera was the perfect choice for a story about social graces!

Then it occurred to Vera that Octavia was as curious about her as she was about the mink. Perhaps this whole free-lesson thing was also a lesson for Octavia. She probably thought she'd find out all about the town from Vera!

The fox sipped her tea and tried to appear as innocent as she could. Her brain was working overtime, though, trying to connect all the dots among the newcomer Octavia Grey, Julia Elkin, the robbery at the von Beaverpelt mansion, and the missing jewels and silver. What did it all mean?

Meanwhile, Octavia was asking Vera questions about her job at the paper. Vera was conscious of sitting up a little straighter in her chair and speaking a little more carefully as she framed her responses, so she supposed this unusual "class" was having some effect.

Octavia moved on to inquiries about Shady Hollow and its recent history of violence. What did Vera think about the police presence in town? Were they competent?

"It's not my place to say," Vera demurred. She was annoyed at Orville, but she wasn't going to stoop to badmouthing the town constabulary because of it. "Chief Meade has been reelected twelve times, and Orville is well known as his deputy. It seems to work, for the most part. I promise that Shady Hollow isn't a hotbed of murder."

"One hopes not," Octavia said, "but so often we can't discern something's true nature until we can see past the surface."

"It's a good little town," Vera said, defending her home. Sure, she hadn't lived in Shady Hollow for very long compared to most, but she loved it, and she didn't want anyone—not even a fancy silver-coated mink—to disparage it.

"It certainly seems so," Octavia agreed. "So different from my own upbringing, naturally, but it has a rustic charm."

Vera had lived in a big city, and she knew a backpawed compliment when she heard it. She decided it was time to take charge.

"Such a pretty silver service," Vera said. "Has it been in your family long?"

"I wish I could say it has!" Octavia gave a little laugh. "I should have a story that it was the teapot with which my grandmother served the king. But the truth is that I purchased the whole set not long ago from a little knickknack shop in a town called Elm Grove. I knew I would need equipment for my school, you see."

"Ah, of course," Vera said. Inwardly, she thought, *Nuts!* It would have been perfect to be able to trace the teapot from the von Beaverpelts to the robber to Octavia. But things were rarely that simple. Elm Grove was close by; the robber must have fenced the silver there shortly after stealing it. Maybe there was a string of owners before Octavia picked it up.

Still, it was funny that the tea set had ended up in Shady Hollow again after all this time. Assuming, of course, that it *was* the same set. Anastasia or Esme would know for sure. Vera had spied a glass-fronted cabinet near the fireplace, which was clearly where the tea service was kept when not in use. Vera feared there was a lock on the cabinet, and she could hardly resort to Lefty-level measures to unlock it. Drat.

"Have any von Beaverpelts been in to sign up for a class?" Vera asked. "Esme is pretty busy with work, but Stasia sounded interested."

"Yes, she's going to attend a dance class," Octavia said, "purely to see it's done right, she made sure to tell me. I'd still love to see *you* in a dance class, Vera. So many creatures around town seem to have taken an interest."

Like Orville? Vera wanted to say, but she didn't want to give anyone the satisfaction. So she said, "I'm afraid that my work keeps me far too busy. In fact, I should be writing an article right now. Won't you excuse me?"

She got up before Octavia could try to dissuade her. "Thank you for the tea. It was lovely," Vera said as she turned to go.

"A pleasure to converse with you. You're welcome anytime, dear," Octavia replied graciously.

Vera was happy to get outside and stand in the cool air of the autumn night. Petits fours were all well and good, but she was simply not the tea-party type. She liked coffee by the gallon and a pastry strong enough to stand up to it. That's how she had made it as a reporter.

She returned to her own home to write up an article on her experience; it would be the introduction to the series about Octavia's school. Vera planned to write the exact minimum required word count for each weekly piece and then never think about them again.

The article was fine, she thought as she read over the final draft later that night. But it lacked pizzazz. What it needed was a hook. Her eyes fell on the book she'd bought at the bookshop. Perhaps she could find an interesting tidbit about the mink dynasty to include. That would spice things up!

Newly motivated, she picked up the book and started to page through it.

Chapter 18

Vera decided that if she was going to research Octavia's family heritage, she was going to do it properly. After making a big cup of chamomile tea, she settled herself on the couch under a blanket with the enormous book of mink history.

At first she merely flipped through the book and looked at the pictures. Lots of formal portraits of minks dressed in fancy gowns and suits and often wearing crowns. They all looked aristocratic and boring. Then Vera's eye caught a few paragraphs that sounded familiar. She remembered Ms. Grey relating a story during the late-afternoon tea about how one of her many relatives came to power: The mink had married the queen of a small principality. Not long after, the queen died suddenly from ingesting some kind of poison—a common fate for many royals. Following the queen's demise, the throne became the mink's, establishing the legacy of his whole lineage.

So far, so deadly. But wait. As Vera flipped through the pages, she realized that this history was about a family named Sabel, not Grey. As a matter of fact, Vera had not seen anything about a family called Grey in the entire volume. She turned to the index to make sure, but there was no listing for Grey at all. She looked up the dynasties from the Carbonia Mountains, where Octavia claimed she came from. No Greys.

The fox sat back as she contemplated what this might mean. Who was Octavia Grey, really? And why was she claiming aristocratic descent from a family that apparently didn't exist? She could be anyone!

Vera would have to say something to BW. She couldn't write an article that she knew to be false. She would speak to him in the morning. Until then, she put the giant book on mink monarchies aside and picked up a history of the Great Gator Wars, feeling as though she ought to learn more about that conflict. Vera had bought it at the bookstore the other night, knowing Lenore needed to pay for the expense of the evening's entertainment. Vera had, however, skipped buying the book on shipwrecks by Wilbur Montague. (If she suffered from insomnia, it would have been the first thing she purchased.)

In fact, Vera slept so deeply that she didn't even make it to her bedroom, let alone read a page of the history. The next morning found Vera Vixen, Shady Hollow's intrepid reporter, sprawled out on her couch with a book spread over her stomach and her glasses on the floor. The fox awoke with a start and then looked around guiltily. She was ashamed of herself for not going to bed properly after changing and brushing her teeth and fur and whatnot. At least she lived alone, and there were no witnesses to report her vulgar behavior.

After she freshened up and got ready for work, Vera decided that she would go immediately to the office and bypass Joe's Mug for once. She wanted to get her boss's opinion on what she may have learned about Octavia Grey's dubious lineage.

The skunk was already behind his desk when Vera arrived at the newspaper office. His office door was open, so Vera felt relatively safe sticking her head in and clearing her throat.

"Vera," her boss boomed. "Come in, come in." In contrast to his usual practice, BW wasn't surrounded by a blue-gray haze of cigar smoke; perhaps he was reserving that for later in the day. Instead he held a mug of oil-black sludge in one paw. Vera assumed it was coffee, but she wouldn't bet on how many days ago it had been brewed. A cigar was tucked carefully behind one ear, ready in case BW should feel the overwhelming need to puff on some inspiration. "Whatcha got for me?"

"I just wanted to run something by you," Vera responded, pulling a sheaf of papers out of her bag and settling herself into the chair on the visitor's side of Stone's desk.

Vera related the history of the ancient mink monarchy in the old country. She moved along as quickly as she could because she could see her employer's eyes glazing over.

"And the point of this history lesson?" he asked.

"I'm getting to that, BW. Octavia told that history like it happened to *her* family. The book lists the exact same history but attributes it to a completely different family! I don't think

Octavia Grey is who she says she is," Vera finished. "I think she's making it all up."

To her surprise, the skunk just threw back his head and laughed cynically. "Octavia embellished a little. So what? Or maybe she swiped a tale from someone else because it was too good to go to waste. What harm is it doing to anyone? Creatures like to read about the romance of royalty, and need I remind you that the newspaper doesn't use footnotes?"

"You want me to include a falsehood in my article?"

"You can't be sure it's wrong—queens are always getting assassinated for political gain, Vera. Maybe it happened like that in two places and you misunderstood what Octavia told you about her origins."

BW's casual attitude didn't jibe with the editor Vera knew. Normally BW got excited whenever he smelled even a whiff of controversy. Questions about whether Octavia was legitimate could fuel weeks of paper sales. But since Octavia was buying so many ads right now, perhaps BW was choosing a more circumspect route.

His eyes narrowed as he thought the situation over. Clearly his inner muckraker was warring with his inner banker. Then he sighed. "For your article, keep it vague. Just focus on the etiquette school. Not so much about her past. Maybe you can address it later on. I'm not saying no; I'm saying not now."

"Sure thing, Boss." Even though Vera didn't entirely like the compromise, she did have a deadline. She gathered her papers and went back to her desk. She would finish the article and send it to the proofers. She had wasted enough time on this already. She really needed to concentrate on what happened to poor Julia Elkin.

As Vera was setting up her desk to crank out the final draft of the article, one of the mailroom rabbits dashed up and deposited a vase of flowers in front of her.

"Hey!" the fox yelped. "I'm trying to work here!"

"So am I," the rabbit retorted. "That's a delivery for Miss Vera Vixen, and lo, I have delivered it! You should say thank you, Remy!"

"Thank you, Remy!" Vera repeated dutifully. "Who are they from?"

"How should I know?" asked Remy. "I deliver folks' mail. I don't read it." And with that, the rabbit leaped away, off to the next stop on his itinerary.

The bouquet of flowers was quite pretty; it featured a mix of chrysanthemums and daisies in autumnal shades. Who currently thought Vera worthy of a bouquet, though? She found a little note tucked into the greenery and pulled it out. She unfolded it to read *Thinking of you*. There was a smudge of a signature below it—she could just make out an *O*.

"Gah!" Vera muttered. Of course it would be smudged! Who could have sent this? Orville? Not if he was dancing with Octavia. Could it have been Octavia, as some sort of lesson on decorum delivered via bouquet?

"Oh, no. Don't tell me I'm supposed to send thank-you flowers after a tea party," Vera said to herself. She didn't remember that rule, and if it was a rule, she was never going to attend another tea party, no matter how many cranberry tarts there were!

Vera sighed. The flowers would simply have to remain a mystery for the moment. She had a deadline!

She put her nose to the metaphorical grindstone and got to work, typing frantically to get all the words written. The din of the newsroom settled into comfortable background noise. Vera barely heard the click-clack of keys, the dozen conversations, and the constant shuffling of papers. She was wholly absorbed in her work.

Vera was still at her desk when Barry Greenfield stopped and rapped lightly on its wooden surface.

"Hard at work, Vera?" he asked. "You know there's a little memorial service for Julia Elkin down at the church in a half hour."

Vera vaguely remembered hearing that news, but she'd put it aside and forgotten. "Oh, that's right. You know, Barry, I'm going to skip it. I never met Julia, after all, and the service should be for friends and family."

"It'd be a small service in that case; she never got too chummy with us locals. But anyway, funerals aren't for the dead. They're for the living, and it's time to put a period on this passage. You should come along. A bunch of us are going—BW is making noise, but there's nothing he can really do to stop us."

Indeed, Barry was such an old-timer at the paper that not even BW's temper could make him blink. Vera considered joining him but then said, "I really do have some more research to do. You go and report back if anything of interest happens."

The old rabbit snorted. "If anything of interest happens, you can read all about it in *my* article that *I* write for tomorrow's paper."

"Spoken like a true reporter." Vera chuckled. "See you later."

After she had finally finished her feature piece on the new business leader of Shady Hollow, Vera tidied her desk and gathered her things. Her mind turned back to the question of Julia's murder and the possible reappearance of the von Beaverpelts' silver teapot. She planned to spend the afternoon on her investigation. That meant a quick trip to Elm Grove to see if she could get a lead on the stolen silver.

A small ferryboat conducted several trips a day between Shady Hollow and Elm Grove. It was operated by an affable otter who went by the name Jonesy. Vera figured she had just enough time to get to the docks and pay her fare before the boat left on its noontime run.

As she rushed toward the river, she heard someone call her name from a distance, but she couldn't stop.

"Later!" she called back in the direction of the voice. Then she doubled her speed and skidded to a stop just before tumbling into the water.

"One fare for Elm Grove, round trip," Vera gasped.

"Yes, indeed, ma'am," Jonesy replied, taking her payment. He shoved the boat off from the bank a scant moment later, so Vera's mad dash hadn't been for naught.

It was a beautiful fall afternoon, and Vera felt sorry for creatures who were stuck at their desks. She was thrilled to be under the lovely blue sky, breathing the crisp air and thanking the powers that be that she was done with her article on Grey's School of Etiquette, at least for now. An assignment was an assignment, but she did not want to endure any more intimate tea parties with Octavia, particularly not when the mink was also offering one-on-one dance lessons to Orville! She had better keep her silver paws off Orville if she knew what was good for her!

Vera trailed her paw in the water and watched the tree branches go by above her head. Maples burned red, elms went yellowy green, and a few mighty oaks had begun to turn bronze. Leaves fell into the water and got caught in the wake of the ferryboat, following along like a fleet of miniature ships sailing after the larger vessel. She squinted at her wavering reflection, then closed her eyes, listening to the sound of rushing water and the snap of the big square sail as Jonesy expertly steered the boat downstream.

Before she realized it, the small ferry was docking at Elm Grove. Vera thanked Jonesy as he helped her off the gangplank and back onto firm ground. Vera did not get seasick, but she always felt slightly nervous when her paws were over water instead of earth.

As far as Vera knew, there was only one resale shop in Elm Grove. It was called Gleaming Gleanings, and it was run by a magpie. She and Lenore had been there a few times just to look around. Lenore was a big fan. On their last visit, she'd purchased an oversize magnifying glass with an ebony handle. Vera had laughed at the sight of the raven's enlarged eye peering from the other side of the glass.

Vera trotted down High Street, where all the town's main businesses were located. Elm Grove was almost the same size as Shady Hollow, but this town lacked a sawmill or similarly sized industry and therefore felt much sleepier.

Vera was pleased that she remembered the location of the shop, a charming little cottage with a blue-and-white-striped awning. As she entered, a tiny bell over the door tinkled and a loud voice welcomed her. The proprietor was behind the counter, greeting customers and ringing up sales.

Vera nodded hello and then decided to browse the aisles before asking any questions. Who knew if the busy magpie would remember a specific item from years ago? She must get old tea sets all the time.

After the fox had studied almost all the items in the small but well-stocked store, she figured she would cut to the chase. If she spent too much time here, she would miss the last ferry back to Shady Hollow and would have to spend the night. She stepped up to the counter, where the bird waited patiently.

"Good afternoon! Stephanie Pippen at your service! Looking for something special?"

"Yes," Vera said brightly, "I'm interested in a silver tea set. A very specific style—engraved with roses and butterflies. Have you seen anything like that recently?"

The magpie made a show of thinking it over, drawing one wing feather along her beak. "Hmmm. Maybe. Can you remember anything else about it?"

"Carved wooden handle on the teapot, and the creamer pitcher looks like one big rose blossom." Vera remembered the sugar bowl being different, but she left that part out.

"Oh, yes. I know exactly what you're talking about," said Stephanie. "That's a gorgeous design from the silversmiths Reed and Bearton. The pattern is called Queen's Garden. Very high-end. Not many in circulation because folk lucky enough to get any pieces tend to keep them forever."

"Have any ever come through the shop? Have you sold any used?"

"Oh, a time or two I've had a piece but never a whole set at once. As I said, it's rather rare. Why do you ask?"

"In fact, I'm a reporter with the Shady Hollow *Herald*. Vera Vixen. I'm working on a story, and part of it involves a stolen tea set. I'm trying to trace its whereabouts."

Stephanie gasped loudly. "Oh, no! I never deal with stolen merchandise!"

"I didn't mean to imply that!" Vera said quickly, not wishing to alarm the owner. "I simply wondered if someone might have tried to sell you anything of a matching description, and if you remember what they looked like."

"Well, my goodness, I just don't know. Most of my customers are known to me, both buyers and sellers. If I think something isn't right, I won't buy it. I'd send that creature packing!"

"So you've never had a complete or nearly complete set for sale in the store. For sure? Not in the past few months?" Octavia said she'd purchased the set in Elm Grove, but perhaps she hadn't bought it from Stephanie's business.

"I'd certainly remember a sale like that! Why, it'd be good for a month's expenses all on its own."

"If there's no creature who might have purchased such a set from you, is there anyone else in town who deals with secondhand silver?"

The magpie puffed out her chest. "Not any legitimate business, that's certain! I've cornered that market. I suppose there could be a private seller . . . but I'd bet my inventory that no one in Elm Grove is rich enough to own something like that. And if they did own one and wanted to sell it, I'd have heard about it!"

Vera believed her. The magpie had no reason to lie and every reason to be aware of the goings-on in her neck of the woods. Vera offered her card to the magpie and asked her to send a message to the newspaper office if she remembered anything else. Then Vera left the shop, thinking hard.

So if Stephanie was telling the truth, it meant Octavia *wasn't*. The mink told Vera that she'd bought the set recently in Elm Grove. But perhaps she got it much, much earlier—eleven years ago, right around the time when Julia was preparing to leave Shady Hollow. But how? The silver-coated mink definitely hadn't got it in Shady Hollow, because she'd never been there. Someone would have remembered a creature as distinctive as she!

Did the robber sell it to Octavia, who then didn't want to own up to purchasing goods she knew to be stolen? Possibly. Even the most aristocratic creatures might conduct business with a shifty individual in order to save some money.

In any case, Vera had to return to the docks to catch the last ferry home.

While the ferry cruised back upstream, Vera studied the sunset and pondered the situation. She had a collection of clues that all hinted at a connection, but she didn't have solid proof of anything.

"Just a lot of stories," she muttered. That was the problem. All she had were anecdotes—tales of Julia's unhappiness, stories of Octavia's family history, Lefty's account of fake jewels, and more. She needed evidence, something to prove those stories true or false.

When Jonesy pulled up to the Shady Hollow docks, Vera practically leaped off the boat and onto dry land. She was eager to get all her notes organized so she could see what sort of evidence she needed to find. As a reporter, she was used to tracking down sources for articles. This wasn't really that different.

Perhaps she ought to speak to Orville after all. She was a professional; he was a professional. They ought to be able to work together for a good cause like finding a murderer! Vera nodded to herself, pleased that she was being so mature about the whole thing. And if Orville was the one who sent the flowers, it must mean he wanted to patch things up, too.

She rounded the corner of Main Street, heading for the

police station. She had just reached the front of the stone building when an all-too-familiar voice stopped her in her tracks. It was none other than Octavia Grey, and she was just at the door of the station. Vera ducked behind the side of the building, listening.

"You can count on me, my dear Orville," the mink was saying in her silkiest voice. "True love is not to be trifled with!" She laughed a tinkling silver laugh and walked away. Orville called out a "Good night" from inside.

Vera remained where she was until long after Octavia went past. She tried to get her emotions under control. *"Count on me"? "True love"?* The very idea of the couple pledging true love to each other after a week was enough to make the fox snarl.

She wanted nothing more than to bolt home and cry. Or possibly to find Lenore and vent. Or to run away from Shady Hollow forever, just like Julia Elkin tried to do.

The thought of Julia made Vera catch her breath. She had an assignment, and a bruised heart wasn't going to stop her from doing it. She resolved to march into the police station and speak with Orville just as if nothing had ever happened between them. After all, he'd moved on. Why shouldn't she?

Vera took a deep breath and left her hiding spot. She took the remaining few steps to the door of the station and then went in, nonchalantly calling out, "Orville? Still at work?"

The bear was sitting at his desk with a pile of papers in front of him. He looked up at her voice. "Vera! Where've you been? Didn't you hear me call you earlier today?"

"Oh, that was you?" Vera asked. "I had to run or I was going to miss the ferry to Elm Grove."

His eyes narrowed. "What's in Elm Grove?"

"A lead for a story . . . or not. Not sure it panned out."

He relaxed. "Oh, you were researching a story? That's good to hear. I kind of thought . . . well, never mind."

"Never mind what?"

"Nothing. I just didn't know what you were up to since I haven't seen you in a while."

"Well, we've both been quite busy," Vera said. "I've been working, and you've been . . ." *Dancing!* she wanted to say.

"Working," Orville agreed with a heavy sigh. He patted the stack of papers. "Seems like every time I turn around, there's more work. Sure could use a break." Then he smiled at her. "Maybe we could grab a bite of dinner?"

Vera almost snapped out a no but then changed her mind. She smiled back. "Sure, why not? We can get something delivered from the Bamboo Patch and eat while we work."

"More work?" he asked plaintively.

"Yes, I want to compare notes about Julia's murder. You have been working on it, I trust?"

"I thought I told you to avoid that line of inquiry." Orville stood up, and the chair behind his desk squeaked as if alarmed to be so close to such a large creature.

"And did you really think I'd listen?" Vera asked. "I do what I think is best."

"You sure do." Orville looked down at his desk, shaking his head. "All right, tell me what you want for dinner and we'll get to work."

Vera was a little surprised that he acquiesced, but she didn't have time to consider what it meant. She pulled out her notebook, ready to ask him some questions.

Chapter 19

Orville pulled out a dog-eared takeout menu from the Bamboo Patch and again asked Vera what she wanted for dinner. Vera almost said "the usual" but caught herself just in time. Orville might not remember her usual, since they were no longer keeping company. *He probably knows what Octavia likes for dinner now,* she thought acidly.

"I'd like the sesame tofu with brown rice," she said.

"The usual, huh? And should we split an order of vegetable dumplings?"

She loved those dumplings. "Yes!"

"Great," Orville replied. "I'll go over there. Back in a few minutes."

While Orville was picking up their dinner, Vera cleared off the big desk. Using the spare plates and cutlery—they were kept in a cabinet for the rare occasions when the police had an overnight guest in a cell—she set the desk up as a dining table. Now, this was like old times. She poured two glasses of water in the station's tiny kitchen. Vera paused after these small tasks were completed. It occurred to her just how much she had missed spending time with Orville. She had not allowed herself to think about it too much before, but it had hurt when he told her they shouldn't socialize. Was it possible that he *really* had moved on? And with Octavia, of all creatures?

Before Vera had time to get too depressed about the uncertain state of her relationship with Orville, the front doors of the station opened again. Orville was back with a large brown bag. Delicious smells were emanating from it.

"Thanks so much for this," she said as Orville moved to the desk and began to unpack the bag. He placed two small paper containers near her plate and two slightly larger ones near his own.

"Everyone has to eat," he noted.

"What do I owe you?" she asked. If they were no longer dating, Vera wanted to pay her fair share.

"Don't worry about it," Orville answered quickly. "You can get it next time."

The fox and the bear ate in relative silence. Occasionally one of them commented on the quality of the food and the other one agreed. There were no personal topics broached and no talk of the discovery of the body of Julia Elkin. Despite the ordinariness of the situation, Vera was enjoying herself immensely and just reveling at being in Orville's company.

When most of the food was gone, Vera flipped open her

notebook and started to tell Orville what she had learned from her investigation. She relayed the discoveries of the robber's hideout and of Julia's suitcase—in the case of the latter item, Vera told him where to recover it. "I've got the letters at my place, airing out by the fire. But I'll bring them over whenever you want."

"Sounds like she was definitely intending to leave town on her own," Orville said. "And it sure is possible that she just had some bad luck in crossing paths with that robber in the woods. I remember that case. Folks were scared, especially since the police never got the slightest clue about who the robber was. He must have hidden there and seen Julia. He either thought she was the law after him or he just didn't want to risk a local saying anything about him or his hideout, so he killed her to keep her quiet."

"You think that's how it happened?" Vera asked.

"It's a possibility," Orville said, "and, frankly, it feels a whole lot better to think that's the way it went down than to think Joe followed her and killed her in a fit of rage. Stranger or friend? If I were on a jury, I know which one I'd pick to be a murderer."

Vera had to assume that Orville was speaking from experience, even though Shady Hollow didn't have very many jury trials. In fact, the town didn't even have a courtroom—during the rare times when a trial was necessary, the church was used and the jury sat in the choir seats. Still, it made sense.

She told Orville about her visit to the von Beaverpelt mansion and their account of the robbery eleven years ago and about her later trip to Elm Grove to search for the seller of the silver teapot. Orville looked interested when she mentioned the stolen jewels and Lefty's role in their attempted fencing.

Orville was constantly after Lefty for some misdemeanor or other and would love nothing more than to nail him for a really big crime.

Vera briefly considered leaving out her suspicions of Octavia, but those were an important part of the case. She told Orville about her tea party with Octavia, how the mink had asked lots of questions about the town, and how she had the stolen teapot in her possession.

Orville chewed thoughtfully on the last dumpling. "But there's no evidence that *she* stole it," he said, wiping his paws on a paper napkin. "I'd imagine that if Edith von Beaverpelt saw a silver mink breaking in, she'd remember! And that's not who she described at all." He tapped a page with Edith's account of the robbery.

"Then how did Octavia get it?"

"Maybe she picked it up from a place she doesn't want to admit knowing about. Every town in the woodlands has someone like Lefty. Just because folks come from blue blood doesn't mean they're honest."

"I'm not even sure she does come from blue blood."

The bear's eyes widened. "What do you mean?"

"Listen," Vera said, leaning forward in her chair, "I was reading through a book I bought at Lenore's store. It's all about the royal lines of minks. There's no family called Grey in it. Not one!"

"Perhaps she's not permitted to use the family surname," Orville suggested. "Some families are snobby. I bet Edith von Beaverpelt would much prefer if folks didn't know Esme works for a living. But since we all know who Esme is already, Edith probably didn't try to get her to hide her surname."

Vera scratched her nose thoughtfully. It wasn't hard to picture Edith and Anastasia objecting to Esme's new job. "Even if Octavia *is* using a different surname than her proper family name, she's still hiding something else."

"Why don't you like her?" Orville asked.

Vera shook her head in annoyance. "There are so many things about that mink that just don't add up. You can't be blinded just because she's attractive and has manners." She went on before Orville could say anything. "It's not like I'm jealous. I just want you to be careful. Octavia Grey is not what she seems."

"Why on earth would you be jealous of someone we barely know?" asked Orville, looking at Vera very intently.

She was saved from having to answer by a messenger rabbit arriving with a folded note. Orville got up to accept it. He read it and said, "Scuffle broke out at Ginger's," referring to a slightly sketchy nightspot by the river. "I'll have to go down there and restore order."

"Oh, then I'll see you tomorrow."

"Can't you wait for a bit?" said Orville. "This won't take long—"

"It might! You just concentrate on your work." Vera decided now was the perfect time for her to slip out. She wanted to discuss things with Lenore, and she was afraid that she was going to cry in front of Orville. And that would not do at all.

Vera escaped from the police station and was halfway to Nevermore Books when she realized how late it was. Lenore had probably already closed for the night, and Vera did not want to disturb her friend. "I'll just see if she's still there."

In fact, a golden light glowed from the highest window of the bookshop, and the lantern by the door still illuminated the front. Vera knocked loudly and waited.

A moment later, Lenore peered through the cracked door. "Who's there?"

"It's me," Vera said. "Listen, I've been working on the case and I need more help."

"Tonight?" Lenore asked, an unmistakable reluctance in her tone.

"How about tomorrow? I was hoping you and I could find time to explore the hideout I found in the woods."

"Oh. Well, if we start out early, that would be all right. I can let Violet open the shop." Violet Chitters, one of the innumerable Chitters brood, had been working as an assistant bookseller for a few months now.

"Great! I'll meet you at your place in the morning!"

After saying good night to Lenore, Vera reversed direction and headed home to her cozy cottage. She tried not to think about her impromptu dinner with Orville and how she had run out on him. What on earth was she going to say to him when they saw each other again?

She started a fire in the hearth, poured herself a glass of red wine, and settled in with her history book. She wanted to focus on problems of the past for a while instead of her own present.

———

The next morning dawned clear but with gusty winds, hinting that rain might be on the way. Vera walked quickly across town. She desperately hoped that Lenore had a pot of coffee brewing.

The raven greeted her friend with a quick "Good morning" and a nod of her head toward the kitchen. Vera could smell the unmistakable aroma of a fine dark roast. Lenore knew her well. What a nice way to start the day.

Vera waited until they were both settled at the kitchen table with large mugs of coffee close by.

Lenore asked, "So what have I missed?"

"Where to start?" Vera filled her friend in on the one-on-one etiquette lesson with Octavia and the ferry ride to Elm Grove. "I can't put a paw on it, but there's something off about Octavia Grey. Why would she say she got the tea set in Elm Grove if she didn't? Why does her family history sound exactly like the Sabel mink family's history?"

"It's a little odd," Lenore agreed, "but there might be a perfectly plausible explanation."

"Orville offered one," Vera admitted, then sketched out the bear's theory.

Lenore tipped her head in thought. "Could be. You haven't asked her?"

"No. Not yet. I can't figure out a way to ask without it sounding like . . ."

"An inquisition?"

Vera wrinkled her nose. "I guess. What if I ask and she takes offense? Then she'll complain to BW and he'll get all huffy, and I'll probably have to write another glowing piece about a stupid dancing class."

"How do you know it's stupid? Have you talked to Orville about it?"

"No! I mean, I've talked to him, but I didn't mention the dancing. And neither did he."

The raven sighed. "I see how it is. Well, it's not really relevant, anyway. You *did* talk about the investigation, I hope."

"Yes. I told him about the tea set and the von Beaverpelt robbery and the hideout and all of it. He thinks the robber might have been the murderer . . . perhaps Julia was in the wrong place at the wrong time."

Lenore mused, "The wrong place . . . that's interesting."

"Why?"

"Because that's something that none of the evidence has explained so far. Why was Julia buried in the orchard of all places? If she saw the robber's hideout in the woods, then he'd have killed her in the woods. And that's where she'd still be buried. Why move a moose from an out-of-the-way place to a place where folks work every day of the year?"

Vera nodded, again grateful to have such a levelheaded friend. "That's true! I suppose it's possible she ran and that's where the robber caught up to her."

"If she ran, why to the orchard? Wouldn't you head to the center of town or to some nearby home?"

"I would try," Vera said, "but it would depend, of course, on where I met the creature."

"Maybe. What you need to do, though, is discover some clue as to the identity of this robber."

"Well, you can help me do that. I searched the hideout, but I didn't have a light with me, and I was in a rush. If we go back there together, maybe we can find something else that will help trace this creature." It was a long shot, but Vera was running out of ideas.

Lenore was game, though. Together the two friends traveled through the woodland on the narrow path that was already becoming familiar to Vera. Lenore flew above, tracking Vera as she trotted over the fallen leaves. Vera was now equipped with a lantern from Lenore's storage closet and felt better about the day's prospects, even though the sky was quickly clouding over, the bright blue losing out to dark gray puffs.

At the entrance to the hideout, Vera waved to Lenore, and the bird flew down in a spiral, landing close by.

"Going to have some weather," Lenore warned. "The wind is fierce up there, and those clouds are ready to let loose."

"Lucky for us, we'll be inside," Vera said as she lit the lantern with a match.

Following Vera, Lenore looked around the interior of the hideout with distaste. Birds rarely liked confined spaces, and dark cramped ones were the worst. She declared, "Ew! I wouldn't hide out here if my life depended on it!"

"Then you'd best continue on as the proprietor of a bookshop and forget your plans for a criminal empire."

"I suppose. What are we looking for?"

Vera glanced around. The glow of the lantern hadn't illuminated much outside, but it transformed the inside of the cave. The shadowy patches in the immediate area were mostly gone, though there was still pitch blackness farther beyond, where the cave narrowed and descended into the earth. "We're looking for any clues as to who stayed here eleven years ago. Something left behind, however small."

The pair began to search. Lenore used her wing to sweep away a lot of debris and loose leaves. They found nothing. Outside, the pitter-patter of rain on dried leaves began to sound.

"Bet you're glad you're in here now," Vera said. "Just think, with a cozy fire going and some sprucing up, this could actually be a very pleasant little home."

"Ugh! Maybe for a fox!" Lenore shuddered. "I'd rather sleep in the rain."

Vera laughed as she pushed some more dirt into a corner. "Maybe this isn't the place to move to after all. I just wish . . ." She trailed off, seeing an odd shape in the dirt. "Wait! What's that? Lenore, get the lantern over here!"

As Lenore brought the lantern closer, Vera scrambled in the dirt to uncover the foreign object. A moment later, she held a roundish metal . . . thing. It was just about the size of her paw.

"What is it?" asked Lenore. "Ew, it's all black and bumpy."

"Just dirt. Or . . . tarnish!" Excited, Vera cleaned more dirt off the lumpy object. It let out a dull ringing sound when she struck it. "It's hollow. Like a bell. Or a bowl."

"Oh, well, that will solve the case for us," Lenore said. (Ravens can be very sarcastic.)

But Vera wasn't paying attention. She was scrubbing away at the bowl, trying to see details. Something told her it was very important.

"You'll need some serious polish to get the first five layers of tarnish off," Lenore said. "If that thing has been sitting around for ten years or so . . ."

The bowl's tarnish was thick, but when Vera squinted at it sidelong she could see the outline of a bumpy pattern: the bowl had been molded to resemble a single large rose.

"Queen's Garden," Vera muttered.

"What's that?"

"This is a sugar bowl that matches the tea set that was stolen from the von Beaverpelts. The exact same style of set that Ms. Grey has in her etiquette school, which is missing its sugar bowl! I remember because I noticed that hers was mismatched. This can't be a coincidence. That tea set was hidden here after it was stolen, and then it turned up again when Octavia came to town. She's got to be involved with this."

Lenore flapped her wing in warning. "Um, hold on a minute, Vera. I agree that the tea set is very likely the same one in each instance. But let's remember that Octavia wasn't in Shady Hollow at the time of Julia's death! I know you weren't living here, either, but trust me, I'd remember if a slinky, silver-coated mink was in town. Octavia isn't exactly . . . bland."

"But she's up to no good!" Vera protested.

"Even if that's true, it doesn't mean she's guilty of murder. More than a decade separates the disappearance and the reappearance of the tea set. Your evidence is circumstantial—at best. You need to be rational about this, Vera."

"I'm perfectly rational. She's not to be trusted! Why does no one but me realize this?"

"No one? Would you be referring to a certain deputy of the law because he danced with her one time?"

Vera snarled at the very memory. "Even when we ate dinner last night, he couldn't stop defending her."

"So your problem with Octavia isn't that she's a suspect; it's that she's caught Orville's eye."

"Ugh." Vera pawed the dirt, taking her frustration out on the ground. "Maybe."

"You need a break from all this, Vera. We found the robber's hideout—that's good work. Let's head back to town. You can find a quiet spot and sort out all these clues. You'll find a new direction for your search."

The cave had been thoroughly searched by now, and the little silver bowl was the sole prize. Vera stuck her head out of the cave entrance. "It's still raining."

"That's fine!"

Lenore left the cave as quickly as she could, and moments later she was in the air. Vera streaked over the ground as fast as her legs could carry her. Normally she was content in the rain. But the autumn air had grown chilly, and she didn't want to get soaked. Lenore flew much lower this time, for the wind had also picked up, making it hard to fly at a higher altitude. Instead she barely coasted the treetops. Vera knew she was there, even though she caught only glimpses.

That was how Vera felt about this whole case: she knew something big was there, but she couldn't *see* it. What was she missing? Where could she possibly stand to get a better view?

The problem, as far as Vera could tell, was that she couldn't go back in time. All the residents of the Hollow who'd lived there when Julia died must know more than they realized, but Vera didn't know how to get them to *talk* to her about it. She didn't know what questions to ask.

She was nearly in despair by the time they reached the edge of town, and worse, she was shivering from the cold and the steady penetrating drizzle.

Lenore fluttered down. "Horrible weather! Let's warm up at Joe's!"

They entered Joe's Mug to find the diner warm and steamy and quite busy for midmorning. They both were served coffee without having to ask—that understanding was as warming as the beverage itself. Vera hunched over her mug and breathed over the surface, making clouds of steam on her glasses. "This is better," she said.

"Being foggy?" Lenore asked.

"Being warm! But now that you mention it, I do feel fogged up. I keep running around the edges of this case when I need to find the center."

"What's the center?"

"That's just it. I don't know." Vera took a sip of coffee,

thinking it over. "Julia is the center. She's always been the center. She was the victim, and she was important to the killer. No one buries a creature unless it matters. So who thought Julia mattered? Who did she know?"

"The friend in the letter, for one." Lenore took a long drink from her mug. "A stranger in town, someone Julia relied on for advice. You need to find who it was and track them down if you can. Maybe they can tell you more."

Vera promised she would.

Lenore looked out the windows. "Still raining," she said. "It probably won't let up till tomorrow." She sounded fairly cheerful about it—for a raven—and Vera asked why.

"Rain is good for business," Lenore replied. "Rain means folk stay inside and read!"

Chapter 20

After the raven and the fox finished their coffees and their talk, Lenore was anxious to get back to her bookshop. As she said, a rainy day could be fruitful, and she wanted to be there to oversee her less-experienced staff. It wasn't raining as hard as before, only drizzling really, so Vera planned to take a walk around town and try to put the clues together. She promised to fill Lenore in on what she figured out. The friends separated at the entrance of the café, and each went on her way.

Vera did not mind the rain so much when it was merely dripping, and luckily for her, the weather made the streets nearly empty, so she could think about the case without being interrupted. She loved her community, but today was all about business, and she needed to focus on what she had learned so far. Lenore was right; Vera couldn't let her jealousy of Octavia get in the way of her logic.

The fox walked up and down the rain-slicked streets of Shady Hollow, past the newspaper office and the bank, past little shops like the florist's and the haberdashery. The dreary sky meant that the businesses would have their lamps lit all day, and the warm glow from the windows made the town shimmer both gold from the light and silver from the rain. The few creatures that hurried from place to place greeted each other with friendly, cheerful words, and in one case an umbrella was gifted to a hare who had forgotten hers at home (the otter who gave it away explained quite sensibly that he was better suited for the wet weather). Vera smiled when she witnessed the exchange. Such a sweet town needed to be rid of the shadow the bones had cast.

She continued on, strolling out of the heart of town and toward the great busy sawmill on the shore of the millpond. The weather never affected the sawmill's schedule, and she could hear the sounds of workers moving lumber about and smell the dust from the gigantic saws that cut the logs floating downstream from the wild northern forests. All the time, the millwheel turned inexorably, the force of the water fueling the whole works. Ripples emanated outward from where the millrace joined the pond. Raindrops pattered down, turning the pond's surface from glass to pewter.

Vera walked past the mill and onward, turning over the facts of the case in her mind. Julia's restlessness. The mysterious letters—one half of a vital conversation. The disappearing and reappearing tea set. How did they all connect? As Vera rounded the millpond and reached the marshier side, she remembered the toad Otto Sumpf and the disturbing events of the most recent summer. His death had started a chain of clues that Vera followed all the way to the murderer. Poor Otto! He had been an important part of Shady Hollow. True, he had been a grump and a provocateur, but he had also been a historian of town events, recording so much of his local knowledge in his diaries. He'd been observant and . . .

"Oh, my goodness! The diaries!" Vera had completely forgotten that she had the late toad's extensive diaries in her possession. Though she'd offered them to the police following the investigation, Orville had soon offered them right back, saying the station's storeroom was too full already. At the moment, they were stacked under her bed. She had not thought about them since solving Otto's murder and was in fact unsure about where they should ultimately go since Otto had no family or known heirs. Perhaps the diaries might prove useful again. Otto had kept a sharp watch on his neck of the woods, and he might well have seen Julia's comings and goings.

With this potential new source of information, she changed direction and hurried back to her cottage. When Vera arrived, she dried off her damp paws and put on a pot of strong tea to get the chill out of her body. And she had to fuel her little gray cells, after all. Then she crawled under her bed and pulled out the large stack of journals. Fortunately for her, the meticulous Otto had dated his diaries inside and out, and in no time at all Vera had located the journal from the year Julia Elkin disappeared.

The fox settled herself in her armchair, a full mug by her side, and flipped through the journal from the year in question. Otto had not been particularly chatty in day-to-day conversations, but he shared a bit more on the page, perhaps because he was the intended audience and he felt like he was writing to his only equal. Vera scanned the pages dated months before Julia's disappearance, and her gaze caught on the word *moose*. The entry was dated mid-July.

On the day in question, while in his home at the edge of the millpond, Otto had been disturbed by a querulous and loud voice. After a few minutes, he realized that the creature, a moose, was lost in thought and talking to herself. He recognized Joe's wife from the café but didn't announce his presence (to use his words: *Why should I, when everyone knows I live here!*). Instead, he listened to her ramblings.

She was speaking in a strange, affected manner, almost as if she were attempting a foreign accent and not really pulling it off. The toad was not particularly interested in what the moose had to say (*Great clumsy beasts, only interested in tiny matters!*), but it was difficult to ignore her as she continued. Something about a city and an exclusive shop catering to the richest of the rich, and how successful she and her friend would be, far away from dull old Shady Hollow.

From Otto's description, to the toad it sounded as if the moose was giving an interview on a long life of success— despite the speaker being in a swamp. After the moose's monologue had gone on for what Otto considered far too long, the taciturn toad revealed to his diary that he cleared his throat and spoke up.

"*You know,*" he claimed to say, "*real monied folk never buy their clothing from shops, no matter how exclusive. They either have items made custom or the designers come to them. They would never deign to go to a store like a commoner.*" Since Otto had lived a very colorful life—a life that included a bit of espionage and intelligence work during more-turbulent years—Vera believed he knew what he was talking about.

In the diary, Otto recorded Julia's reaction with glee. The gasp from the riverbank assured him that the moose had overheard his comment. She stopped talking to herself immediately and rushed off. Otto was relieved to have peace restored to his millpond and resolved to create a few more sinkholes in the marsh to discourage further interlopers.

That was the end of the entry. Flipping forward through the pages, Vera could find no other mention of Julia Elkin, except for in an entry dated the day after she disappeared. In early August, Otto merely noted the fact that several creatures asked if he'd seen her pass by that day. He had not and said so. Otto smugly wrote that no one asked if she'd passed by *before* then, so he didn't feel he had to pass on the story about Julia talking nonsense in the swamp. *That was a very Sumpfian decision*, Vera thought.

In an entry dated one week later, Otto wrote that the townsfolk had more or less given up on finding Julia. The general consensus was that she'd left Joe for parts unknown, and good riddance to her, according to Otto—although he expressed relief that Joe was still in town and that the café would remain open. Otto had always been extremely fond of coffee; the stronger and blacker, the better.

Vera closed the journal and carefully put it away with the others, once again saddened at the loss of the admittedly cantankerous toad. Then she looked at the letters that she and Lenore had found in Julia's suitcase. To get rid of years of mustiness, Vera had laid them out on the floor near the fire so the warm dry air could drive out the damp.

Peering through her glasses, she read the letters again, one by one. Each one was cryptically signed only *Your dear friend*. Clearly Julia and her friend had cooked up some kind of scheme to leave town and make money. And Otto's diary entry revealed that Julia really believed they would start an exclusive shop for the most-exclusive creatures. She would have been greatly disappointed if, as Otto claimed, their presumed clientele never showed up. Perhaps Otto's comment had created some doubt in Julia's mind. Was Julia's so-called dear friend trying to scam her out of the money she put up as her share in the dubious business plan? Considering how Julia had embezzled her share from her husband and the café, she might have grown angry if she thought her friend was a trickster.

Vera's brain began to work furiously. Perhaps Julia had confronted her business partner in a rage, they'd fought, and then the friend killed her by accident. And in their sudden grief, the friend buried Julia where she lay. It would not have been an easy task to bury a moose; they are enormous creatures. Fear of discovery is powerful motivation.

It certainly was a possible scenario, but Vera still had no proof and no idea who Julia's friend was. The friend had obviously wanted to keep their plan secret until they and the money were safely out of town. Vera remembered how Joe couldn't mention any particular friend of his wife's—by the end they'd grown too far apart to have mutual friends.

Vera realized she was close to wearing a hole in the rug in front of her fireplace. The discovery of the entry in Otto's old journal was a major clue, but she still needed more. She decided to go to Joe's Mug both to eat dinner and to ask him some questions. There had to be something he remembered but just didn't realize was important.

The café was very busy when Vera arrived. She had to wait some time for a table to open up. While she waited, she scanned the dining room. It was full of Shady Hollow residents, all eating and talking, laughing and drinking coffee. The suggestion of Joe's guilt hadn't driven his best customers away. If anything, folks showed more determination to support their favorite local coffee slinger and pie maker. Sun Li had guessed that would be the case, Vera remembered. He was right.

In fact, the dinner shift was so busy that two servers were being run off their paws. Usually only one was needed. In addition to Esme—who gave Vera a wave as she rushed by with full trays and dirty dishes—Lucy was there, too. The dark-furred mink usually worked only on weekends when Joe needed extra help; she was a student who waited tables to pick up extra money. Lucy was a natural at waitressing, having a talent for numbers and a sharp memory. She'd been the one to teach Esme all the diner slang. Vera wondered if the part-time waitress knew Octavia. Maybe she could ask Lucy some questions when the dinner rush was over.

After some time, Vera was pleased to see that a small table had opened up in Lucy's section. As Vera settled into a chair and the mink gave her a menu, the fox inquired if she could ask Lucy a few questions about her current investigation when the rush was over. Lucy looked puzzled but nodded and then dashed off to pick up orders and serve customers.

Little by little, the café emptied as the creatures of Shady Hollow finished their dinners and went back to their homes on this misty, drizzling night. After slurping down a cup of pumpkin soup, Vera picked at her fall salad: tasty greens with chopped apples, walnuts, and cranberries. It was delicious, but she was trying to make it last so that she could ask Lucy questions without interrupting the mink's work.

Finally, Vera looked up to see Lucy standing uncertainly by

her table. Vera smiled and invited the young mink to sit with her. Lucy glanced over at the kitchen, judged it to be slow enough to do without her for a few moments, and then sat down opposite Vera.

"What can I do for you, Miss Vixen?" she asked in a quiet voice. After the events of last year, most residents knew Vera from her investigation and reporting in the paper, even if Vera didn't know them very well.

"Please call me Vera," said the fox automatically, although she knew Lucy wouldn't. "I was just wondering if you happen to know Octavia Grey. There aren't many minks in these parts, so perhaps she introduced herself."

This was clearly not a line of questioning that the waitress had expected. She looked surprised but answered Vera quickly.

"The one who started the etiquette school?" Lucy asked. "No, we haven't met. I have seen her around town, of course. She's hard to miss with that lovely silver coat."

"She is striking," Vera admitted, thinking that she'd struck Orville for certain. "Maybe that silver is in her lineage. I've never seen a mink that color."

Lucy chuckled. "Oh, it's not something you're born with."

Vera was confused. In the city, she had heard of creatures dyeing their fur various shades, but here in Shady Hollow, the residents were less trendy. "You mean she dyed it deliberately?"

"Not necessarily," Lucy explained. "You see, my great-grandmother Sadie began life as an ordinary brown mink with fur just like mine—they say I'm her spitting image—but the day she discovered my great-grandfather dead in the barn from a heart attack, her fur turned silver. Almost overnight! I've heard that a terrible emotional shock can do that to a creature. Age, of course, will bring out some silver or white, though not usually a complete coat change. And anyway, Ms. Grey doesn't seem old enough for that."

"Wow." Vera was surprised by this revelation. It was certainly one that she had not thought of. Maybe once upon a time, Octavia had been as dark coated as Lucy.

Vera realized that Lucy had been patiently waiting while she mulled over this information. She said, "I'm a bit surprised Ms. Grey didn't call on your family. Where do they live?"

"In a house out past Mirror Lake," Lucy said with a smile. "I live there on weekends and when school isn't in session. My family doesn't come into town much. They prefer the woods. It's quieter than being in town."

"So they won't be attending any etiquette classes?" Vera asked.

Lucy laughed. "Maybe if Ms. Grey were an actual princess they'd be interested. Minks take a lot to impress, you know. We've all got ermine in our family trees."

Vera chuckled. She could believe it. She thanked the young mink for her help and sent her back to work.

When Lucy left the table, however, Vera's brain turned back to the problem of the murder. There were clues, but they were messy and out of order. She needed to put them all in their places. Then the answer would become clear . . . she hoped!

Chapter 21

The next day, Vera woke up bright and early. She sat at her table and grabbed her notebook. She was going to lay out all her most-recently learned facts and then assemble them.

Starting at the center of the page, Vera listed what she knew of Julia. A moose from the north who had grown increasingly dissatisfied with life in a small town, Julia withdrew from her family and began to dream of a new life. That desire had been confirmed by multiple sources, including Joe and Otto. She drew lines for each of them. So far, so good.

Vera continued with her work. What happened next? She drew a line outward. Julia gained a friend in some way, and this friend was someone who communicated by letter. By letter!

Vera nearly dropped her pencil. Of course! Julia's friend hadn't been local. They couldn't have been, because if they were, letters wouldn't be necessary.

"So her friend was a long-distance pen pal," Vera muttered. She went to the letters airing out by the fire and picked them up, one by one, to see if she'd missed anything. While Vera had only read the pen pal's half of the conversations, it was enough to show that Julia's new friend had a gift for storytelling—and also a gift for keeping their own history secret.

Idly, Vera picked up the envelope one letter came in. The only address on it was Julia's—no help there. Then Vera squinted at a red smudge on the back of the envelope. Something else was written there, but time and moisture had conspired to make it nothing more than a blur.

Looking at the next envelope revealed the same sort of red mark, also blurred. "Bother," Vera muttered.

The last envelope had been folded in half, which protected the back from the worst of the damp. This one had a red mark, too, but this time Vera could read it: CLEARED.

"'Cleared'?" she asked out loud. What horrible sort of place was this creature writing from that letters had to be stamped CLEARED before being mailed? Such repression was abhorrent to a free-living forest creature. It sounded like prison.

"Prison!" The revelation sent a thrill through the fox. *This* was the missing link.

She reread the letters with this idea in mind. Now, it was obvious the pen pal had taken advantage of Julia by planning a scheme to steal the moose's money after getting out of jail. Julia had been easily seduced by the idea and happily joined in the scheme to leave the area secretly and set up shop somewhere glamorous. The mysterious friend claimed to have the connections and the know-how, and they wanted Julia to come along because Julia was a friend when they needed one. So the plan was set. The only catch? They needed money.

Then what? Vera riffled through her notes. Ah, yes, the news of the robberies that summer. The robber showed up in Shady Hollow right around the time when Julia embezzled her own family's savings. In all likelihood, the friend also got out of jail right around then, perhaps only days or weeks before. The friend came to Shady Hollow and took up residence in the hideout by the river, aided by a few handouts from Julia, including the pot made by the company that outfitted Joe's Mug and probably some clothes and the bedding, too. But that wasn't enough for the mysterious friend; they had thievery in their soul, so they started thieving again. And the von Beaverpelts were the prime target.

Vera knew of only one prison in the region: Stonehurst Penitentiary. But how could she discover the name of a long-ago prisoner? Prison wardens generally don't look too kindly on the press, according to some of Vera's old colleagues. Sure, she could write and write, and they'd eventually give in, but that would take too long. If she were a cop, they'd answer her questions right away. It wasn't fair . . .

Vera's ears perked up. "A cop!" she whispered.

Moments later, she was running toward the police station. "Orville!" she called out as soon as she pushed the doors open. "I need a favor."

"A what?" Orville wasn't at his desk—he was at one of the jail cells. None other than Lefty stood on the other side, behind bars once again.

"A favor. Please. It's very important! Hello again, Lefty," Vera added, nodding to the raccoon.

Lefty nodded back, putting a paw to an imaginary hat. "Miss Vixen."

"What are you in for this time?" she asked politely.

"Seems my shipment of jarred pecans had some irregular paperwork."

Orville snorted. "Irregular as in nonexistent. Those boxes were stolen!"

Lefty looked affronted. "You can't prove that!"

"But I can keep you under lock and key for the duration of my investigation!"

"And then what? Those pecans are tip-top! You'll let them rot while you poke around? Think of the waste, sir. The *pies*, sir. That's the real crime, letting those nuts go rancid instead of getting baked into pies and breads and whatnot. I'm an . . . ambassador of taste, sir! That's what! And I won't be treated like a petty thief!"

"Oh, Lefty," Vera said sympathetically. "No one thinks you're petty."

"*Thank* you, Miss Vixen." The raccoon sat down on the cell's bed in a huff. "If only you could convince this bruin of that!"

"Um, Orville, can we talk?" Vera nodded toward Orville's desk. She didn't necessarily want Lefty apprised of her theory.

"Sure," said Orville. He stalked back to his desk and sat down. "Now, what's this about a favor?"

Vera sat opposite him in the visitor's chair. "I'm working on a very important article and I need to find some information about an inmate at Stonehurst Penitentiary . . . the place in the next county . . ."

"I'm aware of it," Orville said drily. In fact, he'd sent a few creatures there over the years.

"Well, I need the information fast, and prisons aren't so fast when it comes to speaking with reporters, so I wondered . . ."

"If I'd ask for you?" Orville looked skeptical.

"Um, yes," Vera said, aware that she was abusing their friendship for a favor. But it was for a good cause! "Would you mind terribly?"

The bear looked as if he would mind, but then he said, "What's the question?"

Vera sighed in relief. "I need to know the name of any inmate at Stonehurst who was released in the month of June or July eleven years ago. Name, what species, and what they were in for."

"That's all?"

"That's all. If the warden happens to know whether any of those inmates wrote letters to pen pals on the outside, that'd be helpful, too."

"Pen pals?" Orville asked, surprised. "Just what are you trying to find?"

Vera produced a few of the letters and pointed to the red CLEARED stamps on the envelopes. "Julia Elkin made a friend before she died—an inmate. I think that creature knows something about Julia's death. Maybe they're the murderer, or maybe they just know what happened. Maybe they know nothing. Regardless, I've got to find out the name so I can find out where they are now. I think that's the link that will make all these clues stick together."

"Okay. I'll send the question and let you know what they tell me. If we're lucky, you might get an answer tomorrow. But more likely it'll be the next day."

"Thanks, Orville! You're a real professional."

"Oh, one thing, Miss Vixen."

"Yes?"

"Until you hear from me, don't do anything rash. *At all.* Understand? Remember what happened the last time you went off to hunt a clue during a murder case."

Vera had been cornered by a murderer, and it had nearly led to her death.

She saluted, saying, "No funny business. I promise, Orville."

Chapter 22

Vera was relieved that Orville had agreed to help her, but the waiting would be interminable! She went to the newsroom and had to avoid BW, who was hounding her about when the next piece on Grey's School of Etiquette would be written.

"Maybe after I take the course on how to politely flirt with someone else's partner!" she muttered to herself. She tried to research another article, but her brain was all aflutter. Until she heard news from the prison, she couldn't do much besides sit on her paws.

She slept badly that night and snapped at everyone the next day. Those prison officials were so slow! A pigeon could've flown there and back five times already.

The time crawled by. Vera went home a bit early, too flustered to work.

While waiting to hear from Orville, she looked over the few belongings of Julia's that she and Lenore had found in the woods. She had been over and over the letters, but she really had not looked closely at the other things she'd pulled from the suitcase. Perhaps she had overlooked something that would provide a crucial clue.

Vera picked up the most-interesting item first: a book titled *The Road to Charmville*. It was not, as she'd initially thought, a travel guide. Instead it offered advice on manners. Vera paged through it briefly, chuckling at some of its offerings— old-fashioned guidance about proper attire and when to wear white. Vera nearly tossed the book aside after almost injuring herself laughing about the mental image of a moose in white gloves and a hat.

The pages fell together, leaving the front cover open. There was something on the front endpaper of the book. An inscription read: *To Julia— Get ready for a moose and a mink to take on the world!* It was signed *Mia*. Vera hopped up and grabbed the stack of letters from her desk. She compared the spiky handwriting in the letters to that in the front of the book. They were a match! That meant Mia, a mink, was Julia's friend and partner in the fashion scheme. Furthermore, a mink most definitely fit the descriptions Vera had of the slinky dark-furred robber from the von Beaverpelt mansion and of the creature that Professor Heidegger had seen in the woods. Dark-furred at the time Julia knew her . . . but not now.

Vera's brain was working very quickly. She ran almost all

the way to the police station. She stood just inside the front doors, catching her breath and looking around for Orville. He wasn't there. After she regained her breath, Vera called out for Orville. The response she got was not one she had expected: she heard Lefty answer from inside his cell. She ran over to better hear him.

"Orville's not here, Miss Vixen," the raccoon informed her. "He got a message from the warden at Stonehurst and stomped off somewhere. He seemed pretty worked up."

"Did he leave the message here?" she asked.

"Nope, I saw him tuck it into his pocket."

Drat. She'd have to track down Orville for the news now. Vera thanked Lefty and wished him well. "I hope you get out soon," she said inanely. Although he was untrustworthy, she quite liked the raccoon.

"You be careful out there, Vera!" he called after her.

The fox rushed out of the police station and then paused when she reached the street. What should she do? She was surprised that Orville had not come directly to her when he got the news from Stonehurst. Then she had a terrible thought: What if Stonehurst told him about a mink who got out that summer? Had he gone to confront Octavia all on his own? Vera knew the police bear could handle himself in most cases, but this wasn't most cases. This was a case in which a murderer thought nothing of burying a moose-sized victim and then strolled off as though nothing had ever happened.

Vera made her way to Elm Street and her destination. She pushed open the door without knocking and walked right up the stairs.

Standing at a table set for high tea was the slinky silver-coated mink.

"Good evening, Octavia," Vera said.

The mink turned and smiled. "Why, it's Vera. How are you, my dear friend?"

Chapter 23

Vera tried not to gasp as the silver mink glided closer. She casually looked around for Orville but didn't see him.

"How nice to see you again," Octavia said. "I was just about to pour some tea. Would you care to join me? One's manners can always use a brushup."

Vera decided to ignore this jibe and merely nodded. Now that she was alone with Octavia, she wasn't sure how to proceed. Obviously Orville wasn't here. Did he go somewhere else? Perhaps the news from the prison led him in a different direction altogether.

She followed the mink to the tea table and again beheld the elegant silver tea set and all the accompanying treats. How did the mink maintain her figure if she ate like this every day? She must have a strict regimen of activity. *Burying a moose would be quite strenuous exercise,* Vera thought.

Vera was also sure the mink knew that this visit was anything but casual. But nothing seemed to faze the creature. Was that her game?

"Did someone ring the bell downstairs?" Vera asked suddenly.

Octavia turned toward the stairway for a moment but didn't leave. "No. It's just you and me, dear," she said, turning back to Vera with a cold smile. "Have some tea, won't you?"

Vera dutifully sipped her tea while Octavia launched into yet another story about her aristocratic ancestors. Halfway through the recitation, Vera realized that the tale sounded very familiar, but not because Octavia had told it to her before. No, Vera had read it in the history of minks she'd picked up at Nevermore Books.

Vera interrupted the monologue. "This is when the minks stopped a war between the boar brothers. I read about that, but the surname of the dynasty was Sabel, not Grey."

The mink locked eyes with the fox, and a dreadful silence fell upon the room. *So much for not tipping my paw,* Vera thought.

"Nonsense." Octavia recovered quickly and tried to laugh.

Vera knew that she had surprised the mink, though. She decided to press her advantage. Still, it would've been nice to have Orville around to provide backup.

"You know, *dear,* this tea could use a little more sugar," Vera announced, reaching into her bag for the silver sugar bowl that she and Lenore had discovered in the cave. Octavia was watching her closely. The mink's eyes narrowed as she recognized the rose-shaped bowl as part of the tea set currently residing on the table. "I think you know where this came from."

At almost the exact same moment, mink and fox both acknowledged that the jig was up. Vera was shocked as Octavia's smooth mask of refinement fell away. She stared at Vera through narrowed eyes, and her paws began to clench and unclench. Vera had to escape before things went too far. She knew what Octavia was capable of.

"You couldn't keep your nose out of things, could you, fox?" the mink hissed, her regal tone forgotten. "But I'm way ahead of you. You and your big slow-witted friend! He and I had a little tea party just before you arrived. Soon the sleeping pills in the tea will begin to work on you just as they did on him! I'll put your body next to his and then set the school on fire. And then I'll leave Shady Hollow, just like I did before."

Vera shoved her teacup away, spilling the little tea left in it. Octavia merely laughed and took another sip of her own; she was already recovering her confidence. "Go ahead, dear. You're a reporter through and through. I know you're dying to ask questions."

"*You* were the brown-coated creature who robbed the von Beaverpelt home all those years ago and the same one Heidegger saw in the woods. They all described a dark-furred creature."

"I was brown! Beautiful chestnut brown!" The mink looked at Vera with a fierce smile on her face. "My coat was *perfect*."

"But something happened to turn your fur silver. When? And what was it?"

Octavia's smile faltered for a moment, and Vera knew she'd guessed right. "Must have been pretty bad," Vera said, encouraging the mink to tell her story. "I can't even imagine what could do that to a creature."

"Of course you can't," Octavia hissed. "It's *unimaginable*. I close my eyes and I can still see it . . . All these years between and still it feels like it happened only last night. I can smell the rock beneath me, granite and iron and copper. I smell rain in the air, because the storms *would not come* that summer—they just lingered as great clouds in the sky. It was *so* hot. Did they tell you that, all your local gossips? When they talked about the summer Julia died, did they say how hot it was?"

"Some did," Vera said quietly. "But *what* happened to you?"

"It wasn't long after I left Shady Hollow, eleven years ago. I thought I'd have some capital after that con on Julia. But I don't know what happened to Julia's money, and the jewels I stole were nearly all fakes, and that silver set was too rare to fence locally. What choice did I have? So I packed up the set—missed the sugar bowl in my hurry—and left everything else stashed in that cave. I went into the woods. I figured I'd find a new village somewhere, sell the silver in pieces, and lie low for a while so I could think up a new scheme. I spent months on Julia, and that was all wasted."

"Shame," Vera said drily. "So you found a new town to hide out in."

"No." Octavia shook her head. "I was deep in the woods, heading northwest, when I came upon a great wide clearing where the ground wasn't even soil. It was rock, solid rock, great long ridges of it, with only a few scrubby little tufts of grass here and there." Octavia's voice grew distant. "I thought I'd lucked out! Crossing the rock clearing would be much faster than cutting though trackless woodland for another mile. So I walked directly onto the rock. And in the middle of that clearing, I startled a snake that had been sunning itself.

"The *thing* reared up and bit me!"

"Bit you!" Vera gasped. Her heart thumped painfully at the thought of such a . . . primeval act. Every creature feared this most of all—the knowledge that despite all they'd achieved as a civilized society, an impulse still lurked within them, one that could undo all their rationality and leave them with only instinct.

"It bit me," Octavia swore, raising her paw in the air, "bit me and let the venom flow, as if I was . . . prey." The mink shuddered, her eyes growing unfocused. "The pain was overwhelming. I froze up. My body would not obey me—I tried to run, but I couldn't. Then I couldn't even speak because my throat seemed to seal up. All I could do was lie there in abject fear as the blistering pain rolled around inside me.

"The snake, whoever they were, must have been maddened. It's all that I can think of. The heat of the day, the intense sun on that boiling-hot rock . . . it turned the creature's mind. So when I stumbled over it, it reacted on some base level. I think even it was terrified by what it had done because it disappeared within minutes. I just continued to lie there, helpless to do otherwise. I thought I was going to die. I hoped to die, just to end the pain.

"But I didn't. I lasted the rest of the day and all through the night. At some point my muscles all gave out and I collapsed, too weak to raise my eyelids, let alone a paw. My throat was too dry for me to call out, and who would hear me anyway?

"The next day I woke up when the sun was already high. I could barely move. I crawled my way across the remainder of the rock clearing to the shelter of the trees. Then I collapsed again. I woke up dying of thirst. I begged for water, and finally the rain came. I opened my mouth and let it all in. I let the water wash over me, not caring how wet I got.

"And when I could sit up again, when I was strong enough to look at myself, I saw that I had changed. Maybe it was the snake venom. Maybe it was the rain. But my fur had gone silver. The color had all washed out. I was reborn, in a new coat and with new purpose. I resolved to survive. At any cost."

"That's an incredible story," Vera breathed.

"Too bad you won't write a word of it," Octavia sneered. "Feeling sleepy yet, dear?"

Vera shook her head fiercely. "Still awake enough to ask questions. Your name was Mia when you knew Julia. When did you become Octavia Grey?"

"Mia Sabel," the mink replied smoothly. "I do have the blood of royals in my veins . . . just not in a way they'll officially recognize. I was raised as the illegitimate child of aristocrats, close to their world but never truly a part of it. I saw all the sparkle and pomp, and I wanted it. So I decided that I had to take what I wanted."

"You became a thief and a con artist," Vera said.

"I did what I had to. I used my knowledge to trick regular folks out of their money. They loved hearing my stories, about being a lost princess or an aristocrat about to reclaim my title. And it was easy to get what I wanted from them. Folk like to help, you know." Octavia chuckled. "The silver coat actually made my work easier. I made up the name Octavia Grey and planned more ambitious schemes."

"But why risk coming back to Shady Hollow?"

"I had a brand-new game," Octavia explained patiently. "I

needed somewhere to test it out, and I remembered this town from all those years ago. And anyway, I didn't think it was a risk. I look so different and, besides Julia, no one from around here ever knew me."

"You came back to set up your so-called etiquette school and make money off all the townspeople by impressing them with your fake lineage and your fake jewelry, acting like a fancy aristocrat when you're just like the rest of us!"

"No one has to sign up for my school. It's their choice."

"You lied about your credentials and you made up half your curriculum!"

"So what? I wasn't going to stay anyway. I'd just be here through spring, after I got some money, and then I was going to be off again. No harm done."

"Except for theft . . . and murder!"

Octavia grimaced. "A curse on whatever rabbit had to go digging under that tree. I couldn't believe the bones surfaced now, after all this time."

"I bet that startled you something fierce," Vera said, remembering her first interaction with the mink. "You had just read my article on the bones when I met you that morning. I saw you holding the paper, and you were so upset, you forgot to act gracious."

"It was very bad timing," Octavia admitted.

"The meeting and the discovery of the bones! If the discovery had happened earlier, you could have avoided Shady Hollow and chosen another town. If it had happened later, you might have already been gone again. But the bones were discovered right after you made your entrance and your big announcement about the school. You couldn't turn tail . . . you had too much riding on the success of your new scam."

"I wasn't scared," Octavia insisted. "I was going to get through it just fine. I simply had to make sure to keep tabs on the investigation. So I made friends with the editor of the paper—he told me everything that was going to print; he was so eager to keep me happy. I made friends with you for the same reason, after I heard about your last escapade solving crimes. And then, of course, there was the police deputy, Orville Braun. I had to know what the law was up to, so it was necessary to cozy up to the cop. It was easy. I played like I wanted to help him get you back after your falling-out, and once I had him dancing to my tune—literally—it was easy to ask him about developments."

"A direct line to all the news," Vera said in disgust.

"I was always one step ahead of you . . . until now."

"Oh, please." Vera rolled her eyes. "I didn't tell you everything. But now you should tell me something before these sleeping pills take effect. How'd you get Julia's body to the orchard? That must have been a lot of work to bury her."

"We *met* in the orchard," Octavia said. "She insisted on meeting me but wouldn't come to my hideout. That should have tipped me off that something was wrong, but I needed the money she was going to bring, so I agreed to the orchard."

"She did come?"

"Yes," Octavia said. "She was supposed to bring her haul along, but she didn't."

"And you killed her."

"It wasn't like that. I know you won't believe me, but I wasn't planning on killing her. I really was going to bring her along for the first part of the journey."

"Just long enough to convince her you were serious, and then you were going to take all the money and leave her."

The mink shrugged. "True. But Julia had an attack of conscience. She knew that I robbed that big mansion, and she got all upset. She said it wasn't right to steal things from the residents of the Hollow. I told her that the rich family wouldn't even miss it and that she was even worse—she stole from her *own* family! So don't look at me like I'm the bad one in this situation. Anyway, she said she wasn't coming with me, that she'd stay with her family. She was going to the police in the morning."

"Silly Julia, telling you that," Vera said sadly.

"Silly indeed. I couldn't let her leave the orchard. There was a shovel lying nearby, next to some saplings that were going to be planted. I saw it, and I saw her starting to walk away. So I grabbed it and just swung up as hard as I could. Hit her right in the middle of the head. Just dumb luck. She dropped right there."

"So why bury her?" Vera asked. "You could have just run away."

"But I wasn't sure who she might have blabbed to. And if there was a body, there'd be questions. But up till then, Julia had wanted to leave Shady Hollow anyway, so I figured if I could hide the body, no one would think murder—they'd think she left on her own."

"You were right. That's exactly what they thought," Vera said.

"There were holes and piles of freshly turned dirt everywhere because of all the planting going on," Octavia explained. "So I dug one more, rolled the body into it, and covered it up. I even planted one of the saplings above it so no one would have cause to go poking around in the dirt. Then I got rid of all the evidence left over and got out of Shady Hollow."

"Her necklace must have fallen off when you rolled the body into the grave," Vera said. "A rabbit found it shortly after, perhaps the very next morning. If not for that oversight, no one could have connected the body to Julia for certain." Vera put a paw to her mouth, covering a yawn.

"Stupid." The mink shook her head.

"Considering your lust for shiny things, it's surprising that you missed it. But then you missed the sugar bowl in the cave, the one that matched the tea set. You should have got rid of that, too."

"I know. But it was too good!" Octavia groaned. "Queen's Garden! I wouldn't have got one-tenth its worth if I'd fenced it. So I kept it. Hauled it around for years. Used it in scams when I needed to impress a mark."

"You really grew into the role of Octavia," Vera said. "You practiced for years, made it more elaborate, used all your old ideas in the new scam. It wasn't enough to fleece individual creatures anymore. You wanted to take whole towns at a time."

"Economies of scale. I'm in business."

Vera blinked and lifted one paw to point at the mink. "No. You're a murderer."

"One does what one must." Octavia smiled at her. "I see you're having trouble keeping your eyes open, dear friend."

The mink stood up, blocking Vera's exit to safety.

Vera stood, too, swaying on her feet. "I won't let you do this, Octavia. You need to give yourself up."

"Never! I'll be gone tonight, and . . ." The mink closed her eyes for a long moment, then opened them slowly. "What's happening?"

The fox smiled. "I switched teacups when you were listening to hear if someone rang the bell," Vera explained simply. "So the cup with the sleeping pills was in front of *you*."

"Oh." Octavia looked stricken. "How did you know?"

"I didn't. But I knew enough not to trust you."

"You trickster!"

"Takes one to know one." Vera gave a little bow. "Or should I curtsy? You're the etiquette expert. You tell me."

With a snarl, Octavia lunged for Vera, but due to the drugs taking effect, she overbalanced and fell to the floor. "Ohhhhh," she moaned in pain.

"Stay there," Vera warned her. "I don't want to bang that pretty teapot on your head, but I will if you make a move!"

"Don't," the mink whispered. "Too . . . expensive." Then her head sagged to the floor and she lost consciousness.

"At last!" Vera gasped. She had to find help quickly, before Octavia woke up.

She ran to the doorway, where she almost stumbled straight into Orville, who looked dazed and had a bump on his head.

"Vera!" he said, seeming both pleased and confused. "What are you doing here?" He rubbed his head with a massive paw.

"She said she gave you some drugged tea," Vera observed. "I really thought you knew better than to let yourself be taken in by a creature like that."

"A message came in that a mink was the creature at Stonehurst Penitentiary all those years ago," Orville explained. "Name was Mia Sabel. I came here because I thought it must be Octavia, somehow. But I thought I shouldn't spook her, so at first I just said I was looking for you."

"And she offered you a nice cup of tea while you waited," said Vera.

"How was I to know that she had sleeping pills just lying around? Normal creatures don't do that! Good thing the dose didn't last too long on me."

"We can talk about this later," Vera said. "I tricked her into drinking her own medicine, but I don't know how long she'll be out. You should take her into custody while she's still unconscious."

"Excellent idea." Orville usually didn't carry cuffs—his scowl was sufficient in controlling a suspect—but he had them now, and he quickly restrained Octavia's ankles. "She can flail all she wants," Orville said. "I just don't want her to get away."

Vera agreed wholeheartedly. She didn't even mind when Orville picked up the semiconscious mink and flung her over his shoulder. It was the last time that mink would get close to the bear! The pair made their way out of the dubious school of etiquette and back to the police station. A few creatures were out and saw what was happening.

"No comment!" Orville growled to the few who dared to ask. "You'll find out soon enough, but anyone who interferes with official police business will get an official citation!"

When Vera pushed open the doors to the police station, she was astonished to find Chief Meade sitting at a desk and looking around the station with an expression of bemusement.

"I called him in as backup," Orville muttered to Vera. Then he said, in a cheerful voice, "Good news, Chief! We got her!"

"Excellent work, Orville." Meade scrambled up to unlock the second jail cell, and Orville unceremoniously dumped the moaning mink onto the hard cot.

"Not exactly royal bedchambers," he told her, "but then you're no royal, are you, Mia Sabel, alias Octavia Grey?"

Before the mink could recover enough to answer, Orville

exited the cell and slammed the door shut. Chief Meade locked
it with a massive key.

"Can I have those keys, Chief?" Orville asked. He took the
key ring and unlocked Lefty's cell.

"What's this all about?" Lefty asked nervously.

"Don't want to risk you getting too close to a bad influence,
Lefty. That mink is a lot worse than you. So keep your nose
clean and stay out of trouble. Next time I'm not going to go
easy on you."

"Yes, sir!" Lefty jumped off his cot, stood at attention, and
actually saluted. Then he dashed out of the station faster than
Vera had ever seen him move. Not even when she'd chased
him had he covered that much ground.

"Maybe Lefty really will turn over a new leaf," she commented, "someday."

"Maybe." Orville sighed. "All I know is that I've got a real
criminal under lock and key now. How'd you figure out she
was the murderer without the news from the prison?"

"Wait," said Vera. "Back up. You knew about Octavia and
you *still* went to the school alone?"

"I didn't know she was the murderer for certain," Orville
explained, "but I knew she was a grifter even before the prison
sent the description. I can sense a con artist five miles off."

"Oh, really?" Vera said skeptically. "What were her give-
aways?"

"Little things. When she first moved here, I went around to
introduce myself, because everyone should know the police in
a neighborhood. When she saw me walk in wearing my uniform, she looked like she was about to bolt. She recovered a
second later and told me I'd startled her. But I'd knocked on
the door and announced myself—she had to know someone

was coming up. And I know the difference between someone being surprised, and someone who's afraid of the cops. Believe me, the reactions are different."

"Why didn't you say anything then?"

Orville sighed. "Because I told myself I must have been mistaken. That mink spins a good story, and I think everyone wanted to believe it because it was glamorous to think a creature so refined had come to our little town."

Vera nodded. "But she was just trying to take advantage of us."

"Shady Hollow doesn't need more etiquette, anyway. We're all very polite. What could she offer?"

"Dancing?" Vera needled.

"Hardly. I went back to the school one time because I thought you might be there interviewing her—the office said you were working on a story—but I just found Ms. Grey. She was all questions—about you, about the investigation, and about my plans. It was a bit too inquisitive, and that got me suspicious again. I wanted to see what she was really interested in, so I made up a story about needing to learn to dance so I could impress you."

"And she was so happy to teach you," Vera guessed.

"Yes, but considering that initial lesson, I escaped as soon as I could. There was no way I was going to subject myself to six weeks of *that*. She's a terrible dancer."

"Really?"

"Awful. A creature might learn some etiquette, but you just can't teach rhythm. She kept treading on my paws but blaming me. And at the same time she was trying to get me to tell her what I knew about Julia's death. Worst dance I can remember."

"You already know how to dance?" Vera asked in surprise.

" 'Course I do. What's so novel about a dancing bear?"

"You've never asked me to go dancing."

"Well, I haven't had the chance yet. I was going to. I sent you flowers to apologize, and I was going to bring it up over dinner at the station, but then you ran off in a huff and I figured the time wasn't right."

"Oh. I suppose you've got a point." Vera paused, then sighed. "And the time still isn't right! I have to write something about this spectacular arrest for the paper or BW will go through the roof." Addressing Chief Meade now, too, she asked, "May I get some quotes from you both?"

Chief Meade gave a vague, blustery comment to the effect that Shady Hollow could always rely on the constabulary to restore order. Orville gave a few more-detailed quotes. Vera already knew which one she'd tag as the pull quote: "A decade is a long time to wait for justice, but in the end justice was achieved with hard work and cooperation from the community."

"Okay, I've got to head home to write the rest of this. See you tomorrow!"

Orville waved goodbye and Vera blew him a kiss, feeling that formal rules of etiquette were no replacement for simple gestures.

Chapter 24

Vera rushed home and began typing frantically. She stayed up all night as she wrote, revised, and polished the article.

It was just after dawn when she ran her typed pages over to the *Herald* office.

"BW! BW!" she shouted. "I've got it! The exclusive!"

At the word *exclusive*, the skunk poked his head out of his office. "What's that? Get in here!"

Vera entered the editor's office and gave him the article. Then she slumped into a chair. BW read through it with a red-tipped pencil, exclaiming his surprise every few minutes. ("What!" and "She did *what!*" And, once, an actual "Zounds!" was hollered.)

Finally, BW flung the last page onto the desk. "Good work, Vixen. We'll print up a special broadside to get this out today. And then I want a follow-up with the town's reactions. That will run in the weekend edition."

"Got it, BW."

"And get some breakfast. You look like you didn't eat or sleep all night."

"That's because I didn't," she said.

"Get out of this office, Vixen, and take the day off. I can't lose my star reporter."

"Sure thing, Boss." Vera left the office and wandered out to the street. She was dead tired and blinked uncertainly in the bright light of the morning. Should she eat? Sleep? Tell someone something?

"Vera!" a voice called.

She looked to see Lenore flying toward her. She waved, watching as the bird landed in front of her.

"I was just speaking with Orville. He told me what happened. Incredible! You exonerated Joe and solved a cold case!"

"Suppose so," Vera said with a tired sigh. "Now I just want something to eat."

"Then let's go." Lenore led her directly to Joe's Mug.

In the café, Vera sat in a large booth near the pastry display case—always a good spot to be. Esme poured coffee with a smile and said, "What'll it be?"

Lenore ordered a hearty breakfast for them both and then added, "Let's get some pie, too, just so we don't starve."

Esme nodded smartly and hurried off to place the order.

Though she was practically falling asleep, Vera reached out and switched her coffee mug with Lenore's.

"Why'd you do that?" Lenore asked.

"Does it matter which one you drink out of?"

"Not as long as there's coffee in it," Lenore said, sipping from her new mug.

Vera smiled. True friends never mind when cups get switched.

The morning crowd started arriving to dine in and to take out. The volume rose as more and more creatures shared the latest news and rumors. Several of them stopped to talk to Vera, hoping for confirmation of the gossip.

She told them what she knew and said it would all be in the *Herald*'s special edition. The main points were that Joe was innocent, Julia had received justice, and the town was spared from ballroom dance classes that would be painful for all.

On Vera's third coffee refill, Orville walked in. Esme immediately poured him a coffee in a paper cup and presented a sticky nut roll to go. "Congrats on making this arrest, Deputy," Esme said, emphasizing *this* slightly. "Hope she's secure in the station!"

The bear nodded. "She's not going anywhere. Not yet, anyway. The prison is sending a detail to take her back, and she'll stay there until a trial—though I doubt it'll get that far. Good riddance! The sooner she's out of Shady Hollow, the better."

Orville smiled at Vera as he turned to leave. "Have to get back to the station to keep an eye on that one. She's tricky."

"You'll do fine," Vera responded, fully confident in Orville.

"Dinner tonight?" he asked in a slightly lower voice.

"That sounds lovely," Vera said, blushing under her coat. Orville was whistling as he strolled back outside.

"Well." Lenore fluffed her feathers. "Looks like everything is back to normal."

"Almost. Excuse me, Lenore." Vera had spied Joe working

in the kitchen and wanted to share some news that she hadn't put in her article.

"Joe?" she called at the entrance to the kitchen. "Got a moment to chat?"

"Time for a break," the moose replied. "Let's step out back."

Behind the humble café, Vera told Joe the few details too personal to print—the fact that Julia had had second thoughts about leaving, that she wore the locket up to the moment of her death, and that the stolen café money might not be lost after all.

"It's possible Octavia lied about that, but with the rest of her story, it makes sense. Julia never gave over the money she took from the café's funds. So that cache might still be hidden somewhere. Maybe even in your home."

"Anything is possible," Joe said. "For my son's sake, I hope there's something to be recovered, though money is no substitute for a parent. Searching for it will give us something to do together. And if we find the money, we know who to thank." He gave Vera a smile. "You never stopped searching for clues, Vera. I know it's just the reporter in you, but I'm grateful all the same."

"It's not just the reporter in me, Joe. It's the friend."

His smile widened. "In that case, let me get you a slice of my latest pie. New recipe: pumpkin-caramel cream pie in a butter crust. For friends, it's on the house."

"Joe, I speak for the entire town when I say you can never leave." Vera laughed as they returned indoors to the warmth of the café and the friends waiting there.

The End

Acknowledgments

Between us, we have constructed a world of woodland creatures who live, work, and murder in a delightful small community. But the creation of the Shady Hollow Mystery series was most definitely a group effort.

At the outset, Nicholas Tulach served as our first publisher at Hammer & Birch, going above and beyond to get our stories into book form and out into the world.

We are eternally grateful to our former boss and current friend Daniel Goldin, owner and proprietor of Boswell Book Company in Milwaukee, Wisconsin. He was one of our first readers and a tireless cheerleader for the books, hand selling them to anyone who crossed his path and stood still long enough. May all authors be so lucky.

We would also like to thank our friends and family who bought the books, attended our events, and were kind enough to tell us how much they enjoyed the stories. This love and encouragement kept us writing and helped us explore the world of Shady Hollow, allowing us to discover new characters and places in every book.

Many thanks go to Jason Gobble, publishing rep extraordinaire, for being awesome. We can never thank you enough for your generous support of these books in particular and for being a champion of books in general.

And we must thank Caitlin Landuyt, editor at Vintage Books & Anchor Books, who gave these mysteries a fresh launch into the world and fulfilled dreams we didn't even know we had.

Additionally, Sharon would like to say: Thank you to my beloved husband, Mark, who believes in me and supports me in everything I do.

And Jocelyn says: A huge thanks to my parents, who raised me on PBS murder mysteries, taught me to love reading, and didn't flinch when I chose to major in English. These books are for you.

And thank you, Nick, for always being there. You are without doubt the best thing to happen to me, and I love you more than cheese.

New from

JUNEAU BLACK

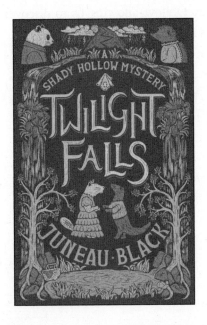

The fourth book in the Shady Hollow Mystery series
sees Vera embroiled in a case involving star-crossed lovers
whose affair may have turned deadly.

"Black's books . . . have become my favorite new comfort reads."
—Sarah Weinman, *The New York Times*

Learn more at JuneauBlack.com

Read more from
Juneau Black

The Shady Hollow Mystery Series

"A cross between *Twin Peaks*
and *Fantastic Mr. Fox*."
—*Milwaukee Record*

(Fall 2023)